FRONTIER BOYS IN FRISCO

I0616748

CAPT. WYN ROOSEVELT

1st WORLD LIBRARY
Literary Society

Frontier Boys in Frisco

Wyn Roosevelt

© 1st World Library, 2009
PO Box 2211
Fairfield, IA 52556
www.1stworldlibrary.com
First Edition

LCCN: 2009923515

Softcover ISBN: 978-1-4218-8898-9
Hardcover ISBN: 978-1-4218-8997-9
eBook ISBN: 978-1-4218-8799-9

Purchase *"Frontier Boys in Frisco"*
as a traditional bound book at:
www.1stWorldLibrary.com/purchase.asp?ISBN=978-1-4218-8898-9

1st World Library is a literary, educational organization
dedicated to:

- Creating a free internet library of downloadable ebooks

- Hosting writing competitions and offering book publishing
scholarships.

Interested in more 1st World Library books? contact:
literacy@1stworldlibrary.com
Check us out at: www.1stworldlibrary.com

1ˢᵗ World Library Literary Society

Giving Back to the World

"If you want to work on the core problem, it's early school literacy."

- James Barksdale, former CEO of Netscape

"No skill is more crucial to the future of a child, or to a democratic and prosperous society, than literacy."

- Los Angeles Times

"Literacy... means far more than learning how to read and write... The aim is to transmit... knowledge and promote social participation."

- UNESCO

"Literacy is not a luxury, it is a right and a responsibility. If our world is to meet the challenges of the twenty-first century we must harness the energy and creativity of all our citizens."

- President Bill Clinton

"Parents should be encouraged to read to their children, and teachers should be equipped with all available techniques for teaching literacy, so the varying needs and capacities of individual kids can be taken into account."

- Hugh Mackay

THE FRONTIER BOYS

By CAPT. WYN ROOSEVELT

This series tells the adventures of Jim, Joe, and Tom Darlington, first in their camp wagon as they follow the trail to the great West in the early days. They are real American boys, resourceful, humorous, and—but you must meet them. You will find them interesting company. They meet with thrilling adventures and encounters, and stirring incidents are the rule, not exception.

Historically, these books present a true picture of a period in our history as important as it was picturesque, when the nation set its face toward this vast unknown West, and conquered it.

CONTENTS

CHAPTER I

ON THE ENGINE

"Would you like to ride on the engine, Jim?" asked the engineer of the south bound train.

"Nothing would suit me better, Bob," replied Jim Darlington. "I guess you can drive this black horse," nodding towards the locomotive, "as well as you did the 'four' that you drove back in Kansas across the plains, when we were boys," and Jim grinned. "Nothing like the real horse," replied Bob Ketchel, "but I can manage this fire eater all right, too."

"Trust you for that," agreed Jim heartily.

"We will be pulling out in about five minutes," remarked Ketchel; "the tourists in the eating house are just swallowing their pie now with an anxious eye on the conductor. Hope they don't choke."

"I'm already, Bob," said Jim.

"No, you're not," replied Ketchel; "go back to your luxurious caboose and get your heaviest coat and your trusty revolver; we might see some game going through the Pass," and Bob winked wisely at his "boyhood" friend.

"Don't pull out until I get back," warned Jim, as he started on a trot toward one of the rear Pullmans, called a "caboose" by the flippant Bob.

"'The General Denver' leaves in three minutes," called Ketchel after the retreating Jim; "wouldn't wait a second for nobody." From the fact that the locomotive was given the dignity of a real name indicates that the time of our narrative belongs to an earlier and more ornate day than this when even the biggest engine gets nothing more than a number.

At Ketchel's warning, Jim quickened his pace to a run, for he would not have missed that ride on the "General Denver" for all the buried wealth he and his brothers had once found on a treasure hunt in Old Mexico. I wonder if an introduction to our old friend, Jim Darlington, is really necessary. At least I am going through the formality. Jim, the leader of "The Frontier Boys," whose adventures began on "The Overland Trail," and were last spoken of in the narrative, "In The Saddle," is now on his way to San Francisco in response to a message sent to him by the engineer of his captured yacht, *The Sea Eagle*. He had been spending the Christmas time at his home in Maysville, New York, where his brothers, Tom and Jo, remained for the winter, much to their mother's joy, but to their own deep regret, when they saw Jim starting out on a journey whose adventures they could not share.

So much for the introduction, now to the narrative. Jim had no time to spare and he could be very prompt when he had to, as all his old friends can well remember. He swung into the black Pullman near the rear of the long train, glided through the narrow alley way between the smoking-room and the side of the car, just missing a head on collision with a stout party coming out of the sleeper. The latter was about to express a haughty indignation at Jim's abrupt approach, but that worthy gave him no chance, as he dashed for section

No. 9 at the end of the car. Here he snatched from his valise his belt and revolver and fastened them with rapid precision around his waist, and then with a heavy sweater in his hand, he made a rapid exit from the car.

Already his three minutes were nearly up, and he had an exasperating delay in the narrow passageway where a file of well-fed diners were coming through. As Jim leaped from the platform the engine gave a short, sharp whistle and the wheels began to revolve. Jim's vacation had not made him fat nor short winded and he sped after the engine, with the swiftness of an Indian on the trail of an enemy. Perhaps Bob Ketchel let his engine take it rather slowly. However that may be, Jim in a few seconds was alongside of "The General Denver" and then his foot was on the ugly saddle stirrup of iron and he was aboard the engine in a jiffy.

"Pretty good for a tenderfoot," grinned Bob. "No wonder the Injuns couldn't catch you."

"It's because my feet are so tender that I take them off the ground so fast," explained Jim.

The fireman laughed at this and his white teeth shone like a darky's from the sooty grime of his face.

"You can have my side of the cab," he said. "It's going to keep me busy firing on the upgrade."

Jim took his place with a pleasurable feeling of excitement and interest. It was a new experience for him and one he was bound to remember. Already the locomotive was gathering momentum. The little town was left behind in the gathering dusk and soon they were threading their narrow iron way through the solitude of the great mountains. Looking back on a sharp curve, and there were many of them on this mountain grade, Jim could see the crescent form of the coaches all alight, where the passengers were seated at their ease.

Then he looked at the intent, grim-faced, young engineer who never took his eyes from the track ahead, keen and quick to act on the first sign of emergency. "They certainly are safe with Bob to pilot 'em, lazy beggars," said Jim to himself, divided between admiration for his friend and contempt for the ease loving passengers in the sleepers, who would soon turn into their berths in comfort and security, while the engineer would guide his roaring, flaming steed through deep gorges, over dizzy bridges, and down the winding grades from some high divide.

Already the night had fallen and all was darkness except where the light from the locomotive sent its fierce thrust of illumination into the night, straight along the steel rails with sudden, quick thrusts as the "General Denver" rounded a curve. "My but it is great!" cried Jim with enthusiasm, as on the engine roared into the depths of the mountains. In a short time the moon rose over the crest of the range, shining with a pure brilliance that the work-a-day sun can only dream of.

After several hours of uneventful progress the train ran into a long siding and came to a gentle stop. It was in the center of a wide mountain valley with nothing to indicate human life except a solitary section house, painted a dull red, and, beyond it a short distance, a water tank of the same color.

"I guess that didn't jar any of those sleeping beauties back there, when I stopped her," said Bob quietly, as he stepped down from the cab.

"Couldn't have done better myself," replied Jim whimsically, "but I would have been tempted to give them a jolt just to make them sit up for a minute."

"Some of the boys do shake 'em up when they feel sort of cranky," admitted Ketchel.

"That's the kind I have always traveled with," remarked Jim, "but what are we waiting here for?"

"No. 10 is due in a few minutes. Here's where we oil up." Jim watched the operation with interest while the engineer and his fireman went methodically from part to part of the engine with their long billed oil cans.

"She must be late," said Ketchel, looking keenly up the track and then at his heavy, open-faced watch. "What do you suppose is the matter with her? No need of losing time on a night like this," he continued.

"Maybe she has been held up," said the fireman.

"That's more likely to happen to us," replied the engineer shortly. "No. 10 doesn't carry anything but the money the newsboy gets out of the passengers for peanuts and bum dime novels but we have something in that express car that's going to California and it's valuable."

"I'm going to California," put in Jim mildly.

"But you ain't valuable," replied the engineer with a grin.

"Except with this," said Jim, putting his hand on his revolver, with a touch of seeming bravado.

"That's where you come in," said the engineer.

"I thought you weren't giving me a ride just for the fresh air, and to get a view of the 'mountings' by moonlight. But where do you expect these villains to jump you?" inquired Jim.

"Well, there are numerous, romantic, little spots along the trail ahead where they might stop us for an interview," said Ketchel.

"I'm thinking they will be a lurking in 'Boxwood Canyon,'" said Bill Sheehan, the fireman. "It's the likes of a dirty black gang that will do the deed, the same that shot poor Jimmie McGuire last month because he wouldn't give up his train to 'em, and him with three childer at home."

"There comes 'No. 10.'" cried Jim, "and it will be all aboard for Boxwood Canyon."

"Aye, but you have sharp ears, I don't hear anything of her as yet," remarked Bill.

"Him has sharp ears and eyes, Bill!" exclaimed the engineer. "That boy there can take the trail with any red Indian and that's the truth."

CHAPTER II

A HOLD UP

At that moment there came a glare of light sweeping down the track from the headlight of "No. 10." With a roar and swaying of the big engine, the train rushed down upon them and swept past with its hind heels or wheels kicking up the dust. Then its tail lights of cherry red grew dim way down the valley.

"All aboard, boys," cried Ketchel as No. 10 passed; "we've got some time to make up."

"He'll stop just short of murder to the train," declared the fireman who knew his engineer when it came to a question of picking up a few minutes of time.

"He will swing her like he used to drive the old stagecoach on the down grade," remarked Jim, "and that will be going some."

Already they were gathering speed, as he sent "The General Denver" along the level of the valley. In a short time the train came to a steep descent through a narrow canyon, and Jim was in for a new experience. Enured though he was to all kinds of dangers it made him catch his breath when the engine went straight for a wall of solid rock and then turned as though to dash straight from the track, into the brawling stream below.

It righted itself with an effort and leaped down the shining trail rocking from side to side and trembling with the vibrations of its fierce power, dashing straight for the depths of the shadows between the towering cliffs. Little did the sleeping passengers realize the dangers through which they were passing every minute.

"Gee!" exclaimed Jim, "suppose a bowlder has rolled onto the track just ahead. It might happen easy enough too."

Just then, Bill Sheehan, the fireman, touched Jim with the end of his shovel to call his attention to something they were coming to ahead. Jim saw a jumbled heap of freight cars half in the stream and half out, and a little ways further on was the rusty ruin of a once powerful locomotive. Jim nodded to the fireman.

"Something has been doing there," he yelled, but the words were blown from his lips and lost in the roar as steam disappears in the air. Jim took a look at his friend, the engineer. He was alert and intent, ready for any emergency, and Jim felt a sense of absolute confidence in his friend's skill. After a ten mile run, the canyon began to broaden out and there were other trees besides the solemn pines. A sense of impending danger came over Jim. He had experienced it many times before and whether it was an ambush of Indians, or the plans of some band of outlaws it had rarely betrayed him. It was something in the air; a vibration that the human nerves are as conscious of as a dog's nose is cognizant of the scent of some wild animal. Jim turned and looked at the engineer, who nodded back at him for a second, with a look that indicated there was business ahead; then his eyes were fastened on the track again.

Jim took out his watch and saw that it was a quarter to two. It brought a quizzical smile to his face. Time and again he had noted the fact that it was just about this time that an attack was sure to come. It sent a thrill through his nerves for he felt that they were rushing straight to a crisis. Much depended on the three men in the engine, for there were many helpless women and children on the train for whose safety they were responsible. Jim noted that the country through which they were going was well suited for the purposes of the bandits desiring to hold up the train.

On either side the walls of the mountains rose at the distance of only a few hundred yards, covered with dark pines and huge rocks showing here and there on the bare fall of some precipice. Between the foot of the mountains and the track was rugged ground, with large bowlders scattered here and there. Clumps of trees and bushes and numerous gullies could be discerned.

It was just the country for a surprise of this kind. Jim stepped down from his narrow seat and got his hands thoroughly warm and pliable, took off his coat and folded it neatly on the seat and stood with his revolver in hand, seeing whether its action was all right. He was a stalwart figure indeed, dressed in his characteristic regimentals, with a thick, tight fitting sweater of blue, pants of the same color, and a new sombrero of a dark hue, for the old one had been battered and worn out of all semblance to a hat, and he was obliged to give it up, though it was like parting with an old friend.

Jim as you remember, perhaps, was a trifle over six feet in height and during his short stay at home he had gained in flesh, so that he weighed one hundred and eighty-five pounds. His hair was brown and straight and his eyes gray.

He was doubtless fit for this battle or any that should come his way.

Just at that moment, Bob Ketchel saw an obstruction on the track, about two hundred yards distant, and applied the air brakes instantly. He had been on the watch for just this thing, and noted that there was plenty of cover where the express was halted wherein the desperadoes could hide.

Slowly the panting engine came to a stop with its nose almost against the stone obstruction and there were flashes from a half dozen rifles on either side of "The General Denver." A simultaneous attack was made at the rear of the train.

It was hardly a fair duel but Jim and Bob Ketchel were competent hands at this game and keeping under cover they managed to get in some telling shots. A near bullet sent a splinter from the cab into Jim's cheek, but he paid no attention to it at the time. When he caught a sudden glimpse of two men skulking behind a clump of bushes trying to get a bead on him, he sent two shots straight at them and then ducked into the cab in time to escape a side shot from behind a rock.

He could hear Bob's fusillade from the other side of the cab and the return volleys from the enemy, but he did not worry about his friend, the engineer, for he knew full well that he could take care of himself. It was the other fellows who would have to look out. But Jim saw a figure leap in behind a rock, near the side of the express car, where he would have the drop on Bob.

There was but one thing to do and James did it. He leaped into the tender which made an excellent fort, and there for a few minutes he kept the bandits at bay. He would have laughed heartily at the fireman, Bill Sheehan, if he could have spared the time, for that worthy had taken up the battle in his own way. Having quickly discarded his revolver with which he was not an expert, he began hurling chunks of coal, wherever he saw the flash of the enemy's fire, and filled with fighting fury he exposed himself most recklessly, but with no apparent harm. Whether Bill's novel form of attack made the attacking party helpless with laughter or because he was in such constant motion that it was hard to get a bead on him, be the reason what it may, at least Sheehan came through unscathed.

For a brief time, the battle was even, in fact the engineer and Jim probably had the best of it, and then there came a change in the situation. The party in the rear, saw that their brethren were meeting with a sharp resistance from the engine, so two of them swiftly and stealthily ran along by the side of the train until they came to the baggage car next to the engine.

Slipping in between the two cars they quickly got on top of the baggage. Any noise they might have made being deadened by the firing going on just below. The desperadoes redoubled their attack when they saw two of their number about to turn the fight in their favor, for it was perfectly clear what an advantage their position on the roof of the car would give them.

They could not be hit themselves even if discovered, and it was certain death for Jim and the engineer for they would not be more than thirty feet from the two desperadoes. Even a tenderfoot would not miss at that distance and these men were not in that class. Neither Jim nor Bob Ketchel were standing so that they could catch a glimpse of the two men who were crawling along the top of the blind baggage. At that instant, Bill Sheehan made a rush for the top of the coal pile to get a chunk of ammunition of sufficient size and weight.

CHAPTER III

JIM TAKES A CHANCE

As Sheehan mounted the coal, he caught a glimpse of one of the desperadoes on top of the car and yelled to Ketchel and Jim who jumped just in the nick of time, and by sheer luck not uncommon in battles, escaped unhurt. As for the fireman he took a novel way of making his escape, by diving into the shelving bank of coal and letting it slide over him. In the excitement of the flurry of firing he was able to do this.

Jim and Ketchel both leaped from the same side of the engine and were protected by a slight cut alongside of the track. Bullets whirred and cut into the dirt around them. As they ran both of them sent a shot at the man on the near side of the blind baggage, with such good effect that he pitched to the ground with an injured leg.

"Duck low, Jim," yelled the engineer; "we will beat them yet. I've got a scheme."

"I'm with you," replied Jim.

This was literally true, for he was right at the heels of the scurrying Bob. As they passed the barricade of stones, Ketchel gave it a quick, searching look, then in a few strides they got to cover in a culvert a number of yards in front of the pile of stone. By the help of a few ties they made a respectable fort.

"So far, so well," said Ketchel, "but it won't do to stay here very long, for they will loot the train."

"Nearly the whole gang is down there," cried Jim, "I can tell by the firing."

"We've got to clear that barricade off the track and quick, too," declared the engineer. "It's our only hope."

"Those stones are pretty heavy to lift off under fire," said Jim composedly, "but I guess we can make a go of it."

"I like your nerve," said Ketchel, a gleam of admiration showing for an instant in his usually noncommittal face, "but I've got something here, that will help us in this hoisting business," and he thrust his hand into one of the pockets of his overalls.

"What is it?" queried Jim.

"Dynamite," replied the engineer, producing a small chunk of the same to view.

"Won't it blow up the engine, too?" asked Jim.

"Not likely with this amount," said Ketchel. "We will have to chance it anyhow."

"Ain't you afraid that you might take a chaw on it, by mistake for your tobacco?" queried Jim in a matter-of-fact voice. Bob Ketchel only grinned by way of reply.

"Now is our chance," whispered the engineer; "keep the beggars lying low while I start the fireworks."

"I'll attend to that," replied Jim briefly and with emphasis.

Then two crouching figures slipped out from the culvert, and Jim kept on the move with the quick dodging motions of a boxer so that the enemy in ambush could not get a bead on him. Flashing the fire of his revolver this side and that at a cluster of rock, or a clump of bushes he dodged on, and such was his accuracy that not a man in the attacking party dared show himself in the open.

Jim was able to keep down their fire, as his ally rushed to the barricade; then Ketchel stooped down and thrust the dynamite into an opening between the rocks and drawing off quickly threw himself flat down by the track. Then there came an upheaval that shook things. A geyser of rocks shot into the air, and in a jiffy Jim and the engineer had cleared off what remained on the track in the shape of debris. The engine itself had most of the cowcatcher torn off and the headlight smashed.

"Spoiled her beauty for you," said Jim. "But we will spoil their game I guess, and I don't think the railroad company will complain at the loss of a cowcatcher." Meantime both had raced back to the engine.

Before the gang had time to fully realize what had happened, Ketchel had regained his place in the cab and had turned the engine loose on the sanded rails. Within a remarkably short distance he had her full speed ahead, with a parting salute of shots from the enraged and baffled "hold ups."

"There goes three of 'em," cried Jim, who had swung aboard. "My what a jump."

They shot from the rear of the train like projectiles from a catapult, rolling over and over down a steep embankment. Two got up very slowly but the third lay as if dead.

"Where's Sheehan?" cried the engineer; "we haven't lost him I hope."

"Gosh! he's in the coal!" exclaimed Jim.

He leaped into the tender and saw a movement under the coal. Working frantically, Jim was able to drag their submerged ally from the retreat that had almost buried him. The cold air brought him to, and he rose staggeringly to his feet.

"Yer started your thrain too suddint, Mr. Ketchel, and pulled two ton of coal over my poor head," cried the fireman in half humorous indignation. "Why didn't you whistle and give me fair warning as to your intentions. And how did you lads escape without bullets in your hides. Yer must have charmed lives the both of you."

"How many of 'em did you get, Bill," yelled back the engineer from his cab.

"Aye, there is many of them that will carry black marks the rest of their lives, where I handed them some chunks of coal."

"The company will take it out of your salary for wasting their coal," remarked Ketchel.

"And shure and they ain't none too good to do it," remarked Bill Sheehan with conviction.

"Get in, Bill, and throw what coal you have got left into that boiler; we have got to make the siding this side of the Divide to get out of the way of 'The Eastern Express.' That little fracas back there cost us fifteen minutes."

"And half a ton of coal," said the fireman, as he bent his back to the work of shoveling, looking for all the world like a black gnome.

"I wonder what has happened to the passengers," said Jim to the engineer; "there seemed to be a lot going on back there the last five minutes of the fight."

"I can't slow up, Jim," responded the engineer, "because we have got to make that siding."

"I don't expect you to, Bob," replied Jim, "I'll go over the roofs. I can make it if those open air burglars did."

"It's durn risky," warned the engineer; "we are speeding now, and the train is twisting so it will sure throw you on some of the curves."

"I've ridden a few bronchos in my time," declared Jim, "and been aloft in some heavy seas and I guess I can manage this."

Self-confidence is all right but pride often goes before destruction and Jim came very near getting his on this occasion.

"And where do you think you are going, lad?" asked Bill Sheehan, as Jim started on his climb over the tender.

"I'm going back to see how many of the passengers have been scared to death and why some of those guys in the sleepers didn't turn out and help us to fight off those bandits back there."

"Oh, them are tenderfeet from way back the other side of the range, they was too busy hiding behind their women folks to fight," declared the fireman, "but you ain't going on no such trip young feller." He made a dive for Jim but that worthy was not to be detained and was half way up the little iron ladder before Bill Sheehan had recovered his balance. "Come back," he cried, poising a bit of coal in his hand, "or I'll bring you back." This bluff did not disturb Jim who was now on top of the baggage car.

"Just like a young limb," he muttered, as he watched the daring James. "I'd have done the same twenty years ago."

Jim crawled or sneaked his way along the elevated part of the roof, so that he could clutch one side or the other in case of need. The train was now winding through a narrow gulch in a line of hills and a fierce wind tore at his body as though trying to fling him loose. He felt that it was more than he had bargained for, as the grimy roof slipped this way and that under him, then there came a sudden lurch and he was lifted clear off the top of the car and one hand was wrenched loose, and in a second his feet were hanging over the side.

His other hand caught the steel rod that opens one of the small windows in the elevated roof of the car. Would it hold? On its strength depended his only chance of life. He drew himself up slowly with every ounce of his strength. The rod bent but held and once more he was back on the roof. So he took his perilous way along and at last he reached the foreward coach. The door was guarded and he came near being shot by the suspicious conductor, who took him for one of the bandits.

CHAPTER IV

THE GIRL AND THE ENGINEER

Indeed Jim's appearance was much against him. He was covered with dirt and grime and coal dust. It was only by holding his ticket against the pane of glass in the door of the coach, that the conductor was made willing to admit him. But when he was informed who Jim was he treated him with due respect and even cordiality. That was pretty good for a conductor in those days.

Jim was an object of interest as he passed through the coach. He might have blushed at finding himself a hero, but if so he was perfectly disguised by his temporary color, which was decidedly dusky.

"Oh, Mamma," cried a youngster, "I'm afraid of that big black man. Will he steal me!"

"Nonsense, Willie, that's the nice, kind gentleman, who gave you some candy at the station yesterday." Jim laughed and the only show of white about him was his teeth. "I don't blame the little chap for being scared," he said, "I'm a bad looking object for a fact."

"You ought to have seen three of those fellows jump,"

remarked Mr. Conductor, as they went on their way through the train; "that was when Bob opened up. I guess one of 'em was badly shook up by the way he lit."

"I saw them take their flying leap," returned Jim, "but was anybody hurt back here?"

"The brakeman got it in the shoulder," replied the conductor, "but I guess he will be all right. Have to take a lay-off for some weeks."

"It's curious how many bullets are fired without hurting anybody," remarked Jim, "but I've noticed that before."

The conductor looked at the tall young fellow keenly for a moment.

"I reckon you are no tenderfoot," he asserted.

"Right there!" replied Jim; "that is if experience counts. But I was born in the East."

"You can't help that," remarked the conductor, to Jim's amusement; "you would have laughed to see them fellows lying close to the floor of the car, when the shooting was going on. It ain't a dignified sight to see a round fat man trying to make himself small by lying as flat as possible."

"I can't blame them," replied Jim; "I would have been trying the same maneuver if I had been there."

"No, you wouldn't," contradicted the Taker of Tickets; "you would have been busy trying to get a line on some of the gents who were kicking up a ruction outside.

"Maybe," said Jim doubtfully.

When they entered the first Pullman, Jim was in the lead and at the sight of a tall, blackened-looking individual entering through the plush portieres into the main body of the car several of the women shrieked, and two stout gentlemen dived down between the seats.

"Conductor!" they yelled; "Conductor! help!"

Jim was greatly embarrassed by this reception, and started to back out hastily, but was stopped by the rotund figure of the greatly in demand conductor.

"Ha! ha!" he roared. "Ladies and gentlemen don't be frightened. This young man is no desperado, but he has been fighting them off down in front on the engine during the late hold up."

Slowly like twin round moons rose the faces of the two stout men from opposite sections.

"I say, Conductor," remarked one of them who was an Englishman, "this is a jolly shame. Can't we travel in peace in this beastly country? Always some bally ructions going on, don't yer know."

The conductor's answer was rather abrupt for he did not fancy the Englishman's style of speech, and that testy individual was more upset than ever. Jim went quickly to his section, got a change of clothing, retired to the wash room and proceeded to get thoroughly cleaned up.

This was quite an operation, undertaken in the presence of two drummers who were smoking and talking in bragging tones of what they had done during the recent fight. Jim was too busy to pay any attention to their talk until one of them addressed him directly.

"Where was you, young fellow, when we was held up back there?" questioned one.

"I was forward," replied Jim shortly. He did not take especially to either of the two men.

"Bet you were hiding under the trucks," asserted the other. Jim did not know whether to laugh, or to throw the fellow out of the window. He had not noticed the conductor who was standing in the passageway, but that worthy had overheard the remark.

"Who did you say hid under the trucks?" he inquired belligerently. The man addressed feebly indicated Jim, then the conductor lit into the fellow for fair.

"You trying to run that young fellow? Why if he took the notion into his head, he could turn you up simultaneous and paddle whack both of you. Why you ain't nothing but—" however, I draw a veil over this part of the harangue.

Jim laughed good-naturedly but said nothing.

After the conductor had left, the men took the opposite tack and were very fulsome in their praise of Jim. Wanted him to drink with them and all that sort of cheap comradeship, but he would have none of their game and got out as soon as he could.

At the first stop the train made, James went forward to join his two friends on the engine.

"And who may you be?" queried the fireman; "you look very much like the Vice-president of this railroad instead of the tramp I saw some hours agone trying to ride the blind baggage."

"I've got my face washed, Bill, and a fresh shirt to my back and my moccasins polished if that is what you are aiming at," replied Jim good humoredly.

"I must say, Jim, it gave me a scare when I saw you swing over the edge of the car, but it was no use for me to try and slow up then, besides I had time to make up, and the engineer can't stop for his best friend then. But I must say you have a cast-iron nerve."

"I felt scared," admitted Jim frankly.

"You had reason to," remarked Bill Sheehan.

"All aboard, boys," cried the engineer. "I see the conductor is waving us to go on. You take Bill's side of the cab and watch me drive her into the Junction. That's my terminus and we will have breakfast together."

"Wish you were going to the coast with me, Bob," remarked Jim. "I'm in for some trouble there I'm afraid, and you are the chap I should want to back me up, and that's solid."

"I'd take you up in a minute, Jim," then he lowered his voice, "but you see there's a girl at the Junction and we are to be married next month." Jim gave his friend a hearty slap on his broad back.

"Glad to hear it, Bob, old boy, and may it be a lucky go for both of you."

"Thanks, Jim," replied Ketchel, and there was a dubious moisture in his eyes, which vanished in a second, as he watched keenly the road ahead.

Jim always remembered the ride into the Junction. The

moonlight had faded from the sky and the fuller, keener daylight was creeping in to take its place. The train was now puffing along just below timber line, and in the west was a semi-circle of snowy peaks, rugged, superb, symmetrical, with the tint of dawn gilding their summits.

On the mountains through which the train was passing were great patches of snow. The air had that marvelous clearness that Jim knew so well and his eyes sparkled, as he breathed it in deeply. Just as the sun came up he saw below at a distance of several miles, in a snow lined basin in the hills, the dark patch of the Junction. As they neared it, Jim's keen eye saw the figure of a girl standing on the porch of a small white cottage. There was something very attractive about the young figure standing there, with the color of health in her face, and a look of fervor in her eyes. A signal passed between the engineer and the girl and then the train roared on towards the station.

"I don't blame you for not wanting to go to California, Bob," said Jim.

The engineer smiled good-naturedly but was content to let Jim's surmise go unconfirmed.

"The boss is shure done for," interrupted the fireman; "he won't be the same high spirited man in a few years he is now. It's all very tempting, but it's like tolling an ox to get his neck under the yoke. It's a terrible thing to see a young fellow like him bent on taking responsibilities he don't know the heft of." Ketchel only grinned at Bill Sheehan's doleful prophecy for he knew the root of it, as the fireman's wife was something of a termagant and the sound of her scoldings had reached other ears than Bill's.

Now came the whistle for the Junction, and the train slowed

to a halt on a long level platform on which lay a six-inch carpet of dazzling snow.

CHAPTER V

THE MENU

That morning always stood out in Jim's memory, not because of any unusual adventure, nor because it marked any period in his young existence, but simply that he felt full of the exuberance of life, after the night's adventure; the very air was intoxicating. That, by the way, was the only intoxicant James ever took. He was glad to be with his old friend, Bob Ketchel, even for a short time.

Then, too, there was the certainty of immediate events of interest as soon as he reached San Francisco, and he felt confident that he could meet whatever might come. His past experiences had taught him self-reliance and he thrilled to the sense of coming adventures. But the fact that he was soon to enjoy a good breakfast had something to do with his feeling of contentment. Besides, he and the engineer were objects of interest in this little mountain settlement, for the story of the attempted hold up was soon common property, and the two were the observed of all observers. This is not unpleasant, as many a schoolboy hero of the football field or track knows right well.

In about fifteen minutes' time Jim and the engineer were seated at a pleasant looking table in a sunny corner of the dining-room, with the whitest of cloths and everything about the table neat and attractive. It was not at all like the Wild West, and it is at the eating stations that whatever of luxury or comfort there is in this wild country is concentrated.

There was a hearty menu of several kinds of meats and gravies, fried potatoes in abundance, excellent coffee in large cups, and smoking plates of griddle cakes with plenty of syrup. Jim ate with an appetite derived from a long fast, and plenty of exercise. The reader can vouch as to the amount of exercise that James had undergone in the past few hours. The dining-room was full of tourists at the different tables, and it was a lively and animated scene. The events of the previous night were the general subject of discussion and Jim was fully aware that he was being talked about. But he was a well balanced chap, and was not the least "swelled" by the notice taken of him.

He and the engineer had a good time telling each other of the adventures that had come their way during the years since they last met. Jim could tell his friend of their wonderful trip into Mexico, the excursion into Hawaii, and what occurred in the Hollow Mountain, likewise of their encounter with Captain Broome, that booming old pirate whose splendid yacht they had seized after a struggle that required strategy as well as bravery. However, Captain Broome was not through with Jim as we shall soon see.

"Well, Jim," said Ketchel finally, as he pushed his chair back from the table, and took a quick look at his watch, "the train you pass here is due in ten minutes and then you will be pulling out. Let's go outside; it's a bit too warm in here to suit me."

"All right, Bob, the fresh air will seem good to both of us."

As they stopped at the office just outside the dining-room door, there was a moment's friendly rivalry to see who should settle for the breakfast but Ketchel winked at the clerk behind the circular counter with its usual cigar case, and porcupine arrangement of toothpicks. "His money is no good, Sam," he asserted, "when he's traveling in my company."

"You're the judge, Bob," said the clerk. "I hear you and your friend were held up in Bear Valley last night, together with the train you were toting along. How about it?"

"I'll tell you later, Sam. Jim here is leaving on No. 7 and we are old pals and have got some talking yet."

"I see!" acquiesced Sam. "Good luck to you," and he nodded good humoredly to Jim. The two friends went out into the crisp, clear air. The snow crunched under their feet as they paced along the platform, and the elixir of the atmosphere made every bit of them tingle with its vivacity and life.

Jim's eyes sparkled and his face was ruddy with the glow of healthy blood in the cold air. He took in the scene about him with an appreciative eye for he truely loved the West and was at home in it. He noted the white smoke rising into the clear cold from the chimneys of the little settlement, the encircling hills of the basin where it lay, all of a crystalline whiteness and the sky as blue, as the snow was white, with an intensity all its own. The fresh engine was backing down to the train as the two friends made the second turn on the platform. "I'll introduce you, Jim, to the fellow who runs this engine."

The new engineer was a short and very solid man of quiet demeanor; he looked Jim over thoroughly in a brief moment.

"Glad to know you, Darlington. Hear you had a run-in with that Bear Valley gang, Bob. Stole the pilot off your engine, eh?" And the engineer gave a silent laugh that shook his whole system.

"You notice we came in on time, Joe," said Ketchel, briefly.

"If we are going to pull out on time, we'll have to start now. Anything I can do for your friend, Bob?"

"Yes," returned Ketchel, "give him a ride through the Red Canyon."

"I will," replied Joe as he climbed into his engine and the train slowly got under way.

"Good-by, Jim," said Ketchel, as they gripped hands; "take care of yourself."

"The best luck to you and the Missus, Bob," cried Jim as he swung onto the train, that was now gathering speed and soon the settlement was left behind as the cars swayed through a narrow passage in the encircling hills.

Jim slept during the morning hours and nothing of peculiar interest happened on the day's trip, though Jim enjoyed every minute of it, especially the ride on the locomotive through Red Canyon, with its walls rising for several thousands of feet in breathless grandeur. Gazing from above, the train must have appeared like a worm crawling along the base of the cliffs.

Twenty-four hours later the huge rounded bulk of the Sierra Nevada loomed dead ahead. When the train came to a halt at a small station at the foot of the range, Jim got out as usual to take a walk up and down the platform. He saw a small box in front of the station supported on a larger one with a curtain in front of it. Upon the lower box was inscribed the legend, "The Famous Rocky Mountain Bat."

Jim was naturally interested in all fauna. (Note the word, youthful reader, and look it up in the dictionary.) So he sauntered up to the cage and lifting the cheap red curtain looked in. What he saw made him gasp for a second, but he did not run, his native courage standing him in good stead. Upon a rich green cloth of Irish hue, was an ordinary red brick.

There was a number of the inhabitants leaning against the side of the depot, waiting for just such an occasion as this. They went into paroxysms of laughter, clasping their knees, or beating each other on the back, and their mouths were opened wide enough to have swallowed the aforesaid Bat (Brick). Jim felt like a fool and a strong inclination welled up within him to punch one of these border humorists, but he put the brakes on his temper and thus kept from sliding any further down grade.

Reaching into his coat pocket, he drew forth not his trusty revolver, but a small diary with a red cover and a dainty ivory knobbed pencil in the small sheath. Dost thou remember, honored reader, when thou hadst one of them given thee to keep the record of thy important life? I bet thou dustest. Perhaps, for ten successive days were daily jottings put down; if very persistent perchance fifteen days were recorded and then you quit. Carried away in the rushing course of events, the little diary was left to wither on the shores of Time.

While this stuff has been recited Jim made a careful drawing of the brick which he annotated with proper data, keeping all the time an imperturbable face under the very pointed jibes of the station loungers.

His work in the interests of Science being finished he stepped over to the place of the scorners, and planting himself squarely in front of the most boisterous of the group, began calmly to make a sketch of this wide-mouthed individual. Instantly the fellow's face grew sober, and the crowd ready for any kind of fun began to jeer him.

This made the man angry and he made a bull-like rush for Jim, who was not prepared for this maneuver and he was thrown from his balance, striking with considerable force upon the station platform.

CHAPTER VI

AN OLD ACQUAINTANCE

The crowd, which was a good-natured one, gathered around cheering its champion and laughing at Jim's fall. But James was thoroughly aroused by the fall, which had added insult to an injury, and exerting part of his unusual strength he struggled to his feet, and caught his opponent at arms' length from him, and then turning him over gave him a few hearty spanks while the crowd roared.

Naturally the man was furious when Jim turned him loose with a shove that sent him staggering back for a number of feet, and he picked up a good sized rock. He came on to demolish Jim with it, but some of his comrades collared him so that he could not do any mischief and the attention of the crowd was diverted to some more visitors to the shrine of the wonderful Rocky Mountain Bat. One was a tall and angular Englishman dressed in some rough looking suiting and his good lady who had on a long ulster and a hat with a green veil accompanied him.

"Aw, and what is that?" he questioned, standing and looking at the curtained box.

"Why, Charles, it says on the box, that it contains 'The

famous Rocky Mountain Bat,'" said his wife with a show of her prominent teeth.

"Bah Jove, we'll have a look into that."

They did and viewed it with closer and closer scrutiny.

"Why d'ye know the beast has escaped. That bit of brick wouldn't hold him. I daresay the villagers will be surprised when they find it has gone."

"It certainly is astonishing," exclaimed the lady. "Do you suppose it can be a joke?"

"Impossible. How quite absurd you are."

Jim who was standing near by looking on with deepest interest, grinned audibly while the overwrought "villagers" could stand no more. They regarded the Englishman solemnly, shook their heads sadly and adjourned to the nearest public house, to discuss the awful density of some foreigners.

"Most extraordinary people," commented the Englishman; "sometimes awfully jolly, and then take to drink because they lose something like a bloomin' bat."

Jim moved away lest he, too, should be driven to drink. He walked towards the train, which was due to start in a short time, taking no notice of anyone. But there was one individual who was keeping an eye on Jim. He had been standing in front of a saloon just across from the station watching all that was going on.

This man was short like a dwarf, and was evidently a Mexican, and the proud possessor of one glass eye. But his other eye was fixed upon the tall young fellow in the blue suit, and the dark sombrero. When Jim was safely on the sleeper, the Mexican did not attempt to follow him but went into the smoker, and puffed at a cigarette; meantime he was doing some thinking and planning.

Jim was soon to find that his old pirate friend, Captain Bill Broome, had a long arm. A dry word of explanation is necessary here. Frontier Boys on the Coast served to introduce this redoubtable man to the readers of this series. The Frontier Boys though badly beaten by the captain at first, finally under the leadership of Jim, out-maneuvered him and captured his ship.

The Mexican who was watching Jim was one of Bill Broome's trusted agents, and the most vicious, if not the most skillful that he made use of in his nefarious business. Jim might have recognized him, though he was much changed by a short, curly black beard that he had purposely allowed to grow and which did not make his personal appearance the more attractive.

However, Jim did not dream of anyone being on his trail at such a distance from San Francisco, though he knew from the letter that he carried that there was trouble to be expected when he arrived there. But for the present he was just content to take things easy and to enjoy his trip, which he was certainly doing. Moreover, Jim was naturally of a frank and straightforward nature and unsuspicious, unless something put him on his guard and then he was not to be easily fooled.

How was it that Captain Broome knew of Jim's exact whereabouts. He was certainly not a confidante in regard to his plans and had no direct means of knowing that James was on his way West. The explanation is simple enough. The news of the train robbery or rather the attempt at it was telegraphed to San Francisco and printed in the usual flamboyant style.

True, Jim's name appeared in the account as Mr. James Damington, but that was pretty accurate for a newspaper and a brief reference to some of his former exploits made identification very simple to the shrewd eyes of old Bill Broome, who was naturally interested in an account of a robbery even if he did not have a hand in it. It was evident that Jim was likely to become as famous as Kit Carson, who performed many of his wonderful exploits by the time that he was seventeen. So it behoves James to be careful. No sooner did Captain Broome's eagle eye see this plum of information about "Mr. Damington," whom he heartily hated, than he set things in motion by sending his greaser scout, with certain specific instructions, to meet and trail Jim.

Once Jim passed through the smoker, but the Mexican pretended to be fast asleep with his hat pulled well down and his head half buried in his overcoat. Jim noticed the reclining figure casually, but thought no more about the man, though his interest might have been aroused if he had chanced to turn quickly for the desperado had raised his head with the quickness of a rattlesnake and his beady eye was fixed with malevolent intentness on Jim's every movement.

That night Jim slept with great soundness as was usual with him, unless there was something to watch out for. As it happened there was, though Jim did not know it. As a link in the chain of what was to occur, I must mention the negro porter of Jim's car. He was an undersized, grumpy person, and Jim had earned his ill will by giving him a call down for his impudence to a lady who had the section across from him.

The darky had vowed to do him dirt, and, though he was

afraid of Jim, the opportunity soon came for him to get even. At one of the stations the Mexican got acquainted with the porter and soon insinuated himself into his good graces, and it did not take him long to find out that this colored person had it in for the tall young gringo, which was sugar to his coffee.

It was a simple matter for him to find out the number and location of Jim's berth, and to make arrangements to get into the car about midnight, so as to carry out his plans. It was shortly after twelve that night, that the porter unlocked the door of the Pullman, and admitted an undersized Mexican.

It was a sinister figure that crouched in the corner of the deserted smoking-room, like a black spider lurking for his prey. At that moment the porter rushed in, and collared the Mexican. The reason was not far to seek. Looking out from the door of the car, he had chanced to see the conductor coming with his lantern; the latter was just opening the door to step out on the platform between the two sleepers.

It would not do for him to discover the interloper in the car, for there would be a riot call immediately if not sooner as the Frontier Boys used to say. The porter hustled the Mexican through the narrow aisle and shut him into the tall thin closet where a supply of bedding was wont to be kept, just as the conductor looked into the smoking-room.

"Somebody in here with a cigarette, Porter?"

"No sah," replied the porter. "Not a living pusson in this heah car but's sleepin'!"

"What's the matter with you?" asked the conductor "you look pale."

"A niggah look pale?" laughed the porter but with mock mirth; "you must be joking, sah."

"Yaller then," replied the conductor brusquely.

He was not entirely satisfied with the negro's reply, and with his round lantern, protected by the steel wires held high on his arm he looked through the smoking-and drawing-rooms which were unoccupied but found nothing. Then he went along the car aisle and into the next sleeper banging the door. Immediately the porter let out the imprisoned Mexican who crouched back into the smoking-room, where he lingered for only a moment.

Then he glided into the dusky aisle of the car, between the heavy curtains with their hanging decorations of velvet bands with large steel figures on them indicating the number of the section. There was the constant roar of the train, and the swaying of the big brass lamps, and from all sides came the loud snores of the sleeping citizens.

Once there came a loud cry of a person frightened by some dream, just where the Mexican was passing and he stopped, crouching low in the aisle. Then as nothing further came of it, he glided along until he reached section No. 9, where James Darlington lay asleep.

CHAPTER VII

WHERE WAS HE?

Jim was breathing heavily, profoundly asleep, and the fellow's first action was to rifle Jim's valise with the skill of an old hand, taking every scrap of paper he could find, a few letters and a memorandum book; these he glanced through; they were not what he wanted, at least the paper that he had been told to bring was not there.

As he shoved the valise under the berth he heard the conductor coming back on his return trip, and he remained as quiet as a frozen mummy, leaning far into the berth and behind the curtain, as the conductor brushed past him. Then he proceeded to the dangerous part of his task. Jim's coat lay under his head, a precaution he never neglected.

With his knife in his teeth, better than a revolver for close work and entirely noiseless, the fellow began slowly and with great cunning to work his hand into the pockets of the coat. He found a long flat letter; this was what he was told to get. Now his cupidity was aroused. He had found nothing of pecuniary value, and he knew that this young fellow carried some treasures of value in the way of jewels.

Jim was too old a campaigner to put these even in the coat on which he was asleep. The spy knew that they must be in a belt around the boy's body. Carefully he located it, and now the lust of theft as strong as that of the Italian for blood gripped him. He despised all risk though he did not lose his craft or caution; he cut the leather belt at Jim's back, and began to draw it by minute particles towards him.

Then Jim was aroused and was wide awake in an instant. He knew that he had been robbed and grabbed for the fellow who slipped away as though he had been quicksilver and when Jim who became entangled in the bed clothes got to the door of the sleeper it was locked. Perhaps he has gone the other way, thought Jim, and he rushed to the other end of the car; the door there was likewise locked.

Jim hated to raise a hue and cry, but he was determined to get the thief. The loss of the belt which contained many of the jewels which he had brought from Mexico was a severe jolt. It would cripple him cruelly in his plans for his coming campaign when he reached San Francisco. At all hazards he must recover that belt.

He went to his berth and slipped into his trousers and sweater and then he found the porter apparently asleep in the smoking-room.

"Here you wake up," cried Jim, shaking him by the shoulder; "I've been robbed not three minutes ago."

"I didn't rob you. I dunno nothing about it," declared the porter surlily. "I've been sleeping all the time."

"You go and get the conductor," ordered Jim.

"I can't leave this hyah car," replied the negro.

Jim's face grew hard with anger, and he grabbed the porter by the back of the neck in a grip that fairly made that worthy's bones crack, and lifted him towards the door.

"All right, Boss, all right, I'll fatch him sure," cried the terrified porter. "I dunno you was in such a hurry."

Jim said nothing but kept watch until the porter returned with the conductor to whom he briefly explained the situation. He looked hard at the porter, who began to protest his utter innocence with great vehemence. "Why, Boss, I wouldn't steal a chicken if he crowed right in my face," he concluded.

"I smelled a rat when I came through this car a time back. You say you caught sight of this fellow when he escaped from your section?"

"Yes," replied Jim. "It was dark of course. But when he slipped through the curtains I got a glimpse of him. He was very short, with a hat pulled down, hiding most of his face, but I think that he had a beard. I reckon he must be in here somewhere for I found both doors locked and I was out in a hurry."

"Here you get in there, Porter," cried the conductor, his face red with wrath, and he gave the negro a shove into the smoking-room, and slammed and locked the door. "That will hold him for a while. I saw that fellow all right enough. He was a Mexican and he got on at Reno."

"A Mexican!" cried Jim, starting back. "No, it can't be, this fellow had a beard."

"Sure! he had a beard!" agreed the conductor. "Well if he is on this train we will get him."

"He couldn't be anywhere else," declared Jim.

"Not at the rate we are going," agreed the conductor. "This is no country to jump off in, especially this time of the year."

A thorough search was made of the sleeper which aroused all the passengers, but the Mexican was not found. However, a trace was discovered when the conductor unlocked the tall, narrow door, to the linen closet.

"Somebody has been here all right," declared the conductor. "I bet he hid here when I came through the train. Something is liable to happen to that Coon when we get to Oakland."

Meanwhile the search was going on through the other cars of the train. Nearly everyone had been asleep at the time and the fellow might have passed through a number of the coaches and not been seen. One woman in the chair car declared that she had seen someone just like the Mexican going through the car, about one o'clock.

Everyone joined in the search, looking under the seats in every nook and corner of the cars. If he was inside the train, it seemed that he must have the trick of invisibility to escape. At that moment, an idea came into Jim's mind suggested by a former experience.

"Maybe the beggar has crawled up on top of the cars," he said.

"He must be an acrobat," remarked the conductor, "to do that."

"I'm going to have a look, anyway," Jim declared. The trainmen regarded him with amazement.

"No, you don't," said the conductor; "that's foolhardy."

"It's slippery as the deuce on top of the cars," put in the brakeman. "I wouldn't risk it myself."

Then Jim's face broke into a grin, as a sudden thought struck him, in regard to the subject.

"It won't take long to find out whether the Mexican gent is enjoying the fresh air on top of the cars," announced Jim; "there's plenty of snow on top and none has fallen for the past six hours."

The conductor hit Jim a clip on the shoulder.

"Long head, boy!" he exclaimed, "I never thought of that."

They went outside and Jim, the tallest of the crowd, was boosted up by a couple of trainmen, between the swaying cars (this was long before the days of vestibules), but they found no trace of the bandit.

"He's certainly not roosting up there," declared Jim.

"Well, if he jumped off, he's a dead greaser," asserted the conductor.

"We will watch and see that he don't slide off at the next station," remarked one of the brakemen.

"He couldn't have slipped under one of the cars, could he?" questioned Jim.

The conductor shook his head with emphasis.

"There's no telling what that fellow mightn't do," said one of the trainmen.

"With the devil to help him," put in Jim.

"To make sure we will search under the train," decided the conductor, "at the next stop."

In a few minutes the train rolled into a small station, near the top of the range. There was a flare of yellow torches under the cars as the trainmen searched every possible foothold, while Jim stood a short distance back so that he could see on either side of the train if a short, dark figure should dart forth to seek escape in the wilds of the mountains; but their quarry was not flushed into the open, even by the flare and glare of the torches.

"Well, boy, we will have to give it up," said the conductor to Jim, when the train started once more.

"It seems so," admitted Jim quietly.

It was hard for him to accept defeat, in this very first skirmish with his old enemy, Bill Broome, and harder still to lose his treasure that was to be the sinews of war in the campaign that had already opened. But Jim soon pulled himself together with rugged determination.

"If I remember right, old Broome gave us a jolly good licking to start with, when he captured us in the canyon in the coast range," mused Jim to himself, "and we beat him in the end."

But the reader is probably asking about the "Mysterious Mexican or Where Did He Go To." Well, friend, I will tell you in confidence that Mr. Mexican was in the train all the time. Perhaps the ingenious reader has already solved the problem of the Mexican's escape, but for those who do not care to be bothered, I will relate what happened, and where he was located.

When he slipped through the door of the sleeping car, which his confederate, the negro, locked after him, he glided through several coaches, where the occupants were all soundly and some loudly asleep, until he came to the forward car which carried a number of emigrants, on their way to the coast.

It must be remembered that the Mexican was a dwarf, no larger than a child. It was easy for him to reach one of the long brass brackets above one of the rear seats, intended for bundles often heavier than he was; here he curled up in his heavy coat, for all the world like one of the bundles belonging to an emigrant and thus escaped detection.

CHAPTER VIII

IN FRISCO

"Well, Jim," said the chief engineer of the *Sea Eagle*, James Darlington's yacht, "Captain William Broome, able seaman, and all round pirate, has routed us horse and foot, taken your riches by proxy and the yacht away from me by his own personal efforts."

"It does look like we were up against it," admitted Jim, "but we have a fighting chance, and I propose to keep on that old codger's trail."

"Good for you, Jim," said his friend heartily, "but if I had a crew that had been worth a tinker's curse, the night that he attacked the yacht, I would have saved that for you! I verily believe that Broome owned several men in my crew, and the rest of them were half breeds and renegades, but the best that I could get together down in that forsaken port."

"I don't blame you a bit, Chief," said Jim; "no man could have done more for me than you did. Have some more of the olives."

"Thanks, I will."

The two were seated in a well-known restaurant, by a window looking down on a busy thoroughfare. It was shortly after one o'clock in the afternoon but the lights were lit, as a dense fog peculiar to San Francisco had filled the atmosphere with an opaque gloom. There is a peculiar attractiveness about a first class metropolitan restaurant. It is a warm and pleasant refuge from the bleak heartlessness and merciless activity of a great city.

Jim, in an unconscious way, was aware of this inner delightfulness of the large softly lighted room, with the noiseless and obsequious waiters, the flowers, the music, the presence of many women, whose beauty and charm made the social life of this remarkable city a brilliant one. Jim was by no means an adept social lion, but he had an outward self-possession that stood him in good stead no matter where he was. The music, and the lights, and the subdued gayety of the scene about him, filled him with a certain elation.

Life seemed a very good thing to him, in spite of his present defeat, and the fact that he was surrounded by very pressing dangers. He would have been a very much surprised lad if he had been told that any of these beautiful gowned women regarded him with any interest. But he carried himself with a simple distinction and poise, that was derived from varied and harsh experiences, that gave him a quiet self-reliance.

James Darlington was not handsome, but he was not bad looking, as he had the power and grace of perfect health and condition. Even the few scars of desperate encounters in the past had not disfigured him, and in his neatly fitting gray suit, which his friend, the engineer, had helped him select, his brown straight hair, smoothly brushed upon his long masculine head, and clear gray eyes, Jim was a pleasant looking specimen of American youth. The chief engineer of the *Sea Eagle*, was perfectly aware of the certain amount of interest which Jim excited even if the boy was entirely oblivious of it. He was a thorough man of the world and regarded the scene which elated Jim, with a cool contentment and a certain appraisal of contempt.

"I do hope that no girl will come along, and disturb the lad's head, he is too good a fighting man to be made a fool of," he mused to himself, as he noted the sparkle of interest in Jim's eyes as the boy watched the diners at the different tables.

At that moment the orchestra in the flower hidden balcony began to play the Mexican national anthem La Poloma, with its enchanting melody, and the well-known strains made a deep rhythmic run through the boy's blood. Outwardly the young masculine has no sentiment, but inwardly he is full of a sense of romance, that he would be shy to confess.

"Here comes the distinguished personage himself," said John Berwick, the chief engineer, "and his fair daughter, Castilians from Mexico, and that accounts for the music. Why didn't they render 'Yankee Doodle,' when we made our triumphal entry, eh, James?"

Jim merely grinned at his companion, and then his face sobered, and his eyes opened wide. The new arrivals were by no means strangers to him. The gentleman was tall and distinguished looking with white mustachios, while his daughter was very dark after the Spanish type; the sheen of her hair like that of a raven's wing, and her complexion of a pellucid pallor, while her dark eyes had depth, and not merely surface.

Under the obsequious guidance of the head waiter, they passed directly by the table where Jim and John Berwick were seated, so close indeed that the flutter of the senorita's mantilla brushed Jim's arm. At the second table beyond they were assigned places, the senor facing Jim. In a way this was a relief to the youth, for he was terribly confused at the sight of the girl and he was afforded time to collect his wits. The senor did not even give a casual glance around, but confined his attention to the menu.

"Old friends, Jim?" asked Berwick who was quick to note the lad's perturbation.

"Why, yes," answered Jim, "there can be no doubt about it. I have told you about our adventure in Mexico, where we saved the Senorita Cordova from Cal Jenkins and his gang and were entertained at the castle by her father. Well, there they are. I hardly think the senorita would recognize me. It seems a long time ago."

"Don't you flatter yourself on that point," said the engineer. "Let her once get a square look at you, and she will know you all right enough. She had an uneasy suspicion when she went past, that she had seen the distinguished gentleman with his back to her somewhere. She would like to turn around now. What did I tell you, she has dropped her fan."

"You must have eyes in the back of your head," remarked James, "but the waiter has picked it up."

"She smiles very sweetly in thanks," improvised the engineer, "but she would like to swat him with it. These dear creatures are not as sweet as they sometimes appear. Have you still the rose she gave you in the castle in Spain—I mean Mexico?"

"Why, I didn't tell you about that did I?" asked the simple Jim. John Berwick doubled over with silent laughter.

"You did not need to tell me," he said when he got his breath; "that method is as old as the daughters of Eve."

"I guess I will go and introduce myself," said Jim hurriedly. "Come on, Berwick."

"Hold on, Jim," said the engineer, "I don't think that is the wisest plan. It makes it awkward for both sides, and people don't like to have their lunch broken in on. We will wait for them in the lobby, or find out at what hotel they are stopping and you can send up your card."

"You are coming, too, to call on them," said Jim impulsively; "I want them to meet you." But John Berwick shook his head with slow emphasis and decision.

"Nay, nay, James," he said, "I have a very susceptible heart. I might become enamored with the fair senorita, that would be trouble, sequel two ex-friends on the sea sands by moonlight, two revolvers flashing at the signal, two beautiful corpses stretched out on the sad sea sands, then slow music, all on account of a girl with dark hair who once wore a red rose in it. Life to me is too interesting for any such nonsense."

Jim laughed at his friend's way of expressing himself, and tried to make him change his mind about the proposed call, but an older man would have told him that there was much sound sense under John Berwick's odd humor. The truth was that the more experienced man of the world knew that the real danger lay in the senorita's caring for him instead of the more simple and straightforward Jim. Berwick knew that it was social experience and knowledge that was apt to count for most in such matters.

"Lucky this isn't our busy day," remarked the engineer, as they waited for the Senor da Cordova and his daughter to finish their lunch.

"It's Broome's move, anyway," replied Jim.

Just then there was an incident at the other table that invited their attention.

CHAPTER IX

THE WATCHER

The Senorita da Cordova, had suddenly leaned forward in an animated manner and spoke to her father indicating at the same time someone who was standing under an awning on the other side of the thoroughfare. Whether the man's presence caused her fright, or mere excitement it was hard to tell.

"There he is, there he is!" she was heard to exclaim.

Jim followed the direction of her glance, and immediately he jumped to his feet.

"Come on, Berwick," he cried, "we want that fellow across the street."

Berwick was puzzled but he knew that Jim was no alarmist who would start on a wild goose chase, without rhyme or reason. He saw the figure across the way but did not recognize who it was. Thrusting a bill into the waiter's hands, a procedure the waiter did not resent, he followed Jim out of the restaurant. As their sudden departure made a slight commotion, the senorita turned her head and got a fair look at Jim. A flush of surprise came into her face, and her dark eyes opened wide.

"Why, Father, look at the tall American going out," she whispered; "it is the senor who saved me from the bandits."

"There are other tall Americans," he said with a smile; "there was a resemblance but that happens frequently in life, my daughter, the other man bore no resemblance to his brothers." The senorita shook her dark head with emphasis.

"It was not nice of Senor James to run away from us, as though we had the plague; it was certainly very far from nice, and I shall make him pay some day."

"Senor James," exclaimed her father, a slight frown on his brow; "you certainly have a remarkable memory, Marie."

"It is not at all wonderful, Father," replied the girl with much spirit; "did he not save me from that terrible Senor Jenkins and his band? I shall remember him as long as there is the breath of life in my little body."

"His memory does not seem to be as retentive as yours," said her father with quiet sarcasm. The senorita's face flushed at this thrust and she sat moodily silent for a while, then something happened which changed the current of her interest.

"Look," she cried, "the man across the street is running. What can be the matter?"

"It is your friend, Senor James, and his comrade is the matter," remarked her father.

Sure enough the two were in fast pursuit of, "the man across the street," and then they turned a corner but crossing to the further side of the thoroughfare they were still in view.

"Oh, dear!" cried the senorita, "I wish I could be informed as to what all this commotion is about and know who will win."

Let us follow them, and perhaps we shall find out. I daresay the astute reader has already guessed the name of the gentleman who caused this distinct and sudden interest and flung consternation and activity into two separate groups. As James Darlington followed the glance of the young girl, he had recognized the dwarfish figure of the Mexican who had robbed him of his treasure and who had previously led him and his party into dire trouble—hence his excitement, but why the interest of the Senorita da Cordova?—Ah! that is another tale, but now to tell the story of the chase, for upon the result much would depend.

"Take your hat and coat, Jim!" warned John Berwick, as the two rushed from the restaurant.

"I won't bother with my overcoat!" shouted Jim; "I'm going to catch that fellow now!"

"Take care of his coat!" cried Berwick to the boy in the lobby, tossing him a quarter.

Then the two friends were outside in the foggy street, where phantom street cars and passersby were moving through the thick white density that had rolled in from the Pacific.

"Just wait here, James," said the engineer, as they stood sheltered by the corner of the building from observation. "He don't know me from Adam and I'll just saunter up and collar him."

"No, John," said Jim decidedly, "I'm just aching to get my

hands on him!"

Another reason which he was too wise to give, was that this same Mexican was a most dangerous animal to handle even if taken unawares, and he preferred to run the risk himself.

"I don't wish to spoil your game, Jim," replied Berwick, "so I will just saunter along this side, and capture him if he escapes your clutches."

"All right," said Jim, "but he is a wary old fox and some of his pals may be on the lookout too, so you had better stay here until you see me on the other side of the street; I am not going directly across."

Jim was too old a campaigner to make a wild rush at his quarry and thus run a chance of losing him in the shuffle. Then, too, he had a wholesome regard for the cunning of his enemy, who was not to be easily trapped. Accordingly Jim, instead of crossing the street, went down around the next block.

In a short time Berwick saw a tall figure, with a black sombrero, emerge from the fog down the street, walking casually along as if not particularly interested in any of the landscape, but out of the corner of his eye he watched the short, sinister-looking fellow he was after. By some obscure instinct the Mexican scented danger and started up the street, and Jim quickened his pace, as Berwick came around the corner where he had been concealed. Instantly the Mexican took the alarm and started on the run, but Jim was like a lion unleashed for his prey; in another leap he would have felled the rascal to the earth, but the Mexican, handicapped as to speed, knew the city as hand to glove, especially every by-way, crooked lane, or devious alley.

His knowledge stood him in good stead now; he swerved into a narrow passageway between two buildings, that was shut off from the street by a wooden gate, which at this moment was left unfastened; this was not by accident, either. Before Jim could turn, the fellow had turned the wooden button fastening the door.

Jim was furious at this escape, almost under his fingers, and his pleasure was not increased when he heard a gentle voice from the other side of the gate: "Good-by, Senor Gringo, I cannot wait here all the afternoon. I have some money to spend." Jim with one bound threw his one hundred and eighty odd pounds against the obstruction. There was a splintering crash, and then Jim tore into the alleyway followed a moment later by his comrade.

At the sound, a fat policeman a block away started on a waddling run to find the cause of the outbreak, and the father and daughter who were watching from the window of the restaurant were more than interested.

"Ah, Mother of Mercies!" cried the girl, "he will be killed." Then she could not help exclaiming in admiration, "What strength! It is Senor James, as I told you, Father."

"You may be right, my daughter," he admitted; "this Americana is very brave and strong, but I trust he will not get himself disliked by killing this Manuel del Garrote, who is of importance not in keeping with his size."

"He had not better come into my presence if he harms the Senor," said the Senorita da Cordova with a bitter emphasis, which her dark eyes endorsed.

"You must learn, my daughter, that in great enterprises we cannot always choose our associates."

* * * * *

When Jim tore through into the passageway between two brick walls, he saw the Mexican dodging around the corner of one of the buildings about a hundred and fifty feet ahead. It did not take Jim many seconds to reach the same corner, and although the rascal was nowhere in sight, the way of his escape was plain.

Opening from the areaway back of the buildings was another gate, that the fleeing Mexican had not time to close; beyond was the blank wall of fog filling the side street with soft gray density. In much less time than I write it, James was out through the gate on to the lustrous black sidewalk, polished with the moisture. But once again the man made his escape and it seemed this time that it was for good. There was a four-wheeler standing near the curb, into which the fellow plunged, and the driver, without a word, gave his two rusty blacks the whip and away they dashed.

Jim was just in time to see the dwarf jump into the coupe. He did not stop with his mouth open, but set out undaunted to overtake the fugitive; neither was he distanced, for Jim had not stayed in the effete East long enough to get pursy and to lose his wind.

Now it was different with the engineer, John Berwick. He was lithe and active enough, and at a hundred yards, was no doubt faster than his friend Jim, but he knew that he was not equal to a cross-city run of several miles in the wake of a four-wheeler drawn by two sturdy mustangs.

CHAPTER X

THE CHASE BEGINS

At the corner of a street stood a hack to which was hitched a big black, and the rusty-looking individual who held the reins was anxious for immediate service. "Right this way, gents!" he yelled, as he noted the signs of a chase. "I'll catch Bill Durnell's team if I bust a wheel."

"Five dollars if you do," cried John Berwick, as he and Jim leaped into the musty interior of the cab. Before they were fairly inside the vehicle was in motion. The driver hit his horse a clip, and away the hack rattled and jounced in furious pursuit, making racket enough for ten ordinary carts. The noise of the wheels upon the cobbles aroused the immediate interest of the street urchins on both sides of the thorough-fare. They threw compliments as well as stones. One, quicker than the others, managed to get a perilous hold on the back of the vehicle, only to be hurled sprawling on the hard road as the hack whirled around a corner on two wheels. He stayed there for a few seconds, with a pained and surprised look on his befreckled face, then he jumped up and fired a rock from the gutter that swatted the coach squarely making a big dent in the black expanse of back.

"I'll break ye for that ye little gutter snipe," yelled the

infuriated driver standing up on his box.

"Yer ought to drive a coal wagon, you chump," retorted the urchin with a shrill yell.

"He's been to a wake," greeted another crowd of boys, who stretched an audacious line across the street directly in front of the surging gallop of the black horse. This time the driver got some revenge by lashing a couple of them with his long whip. This provoked a volley of stones, causing Jim and his friend to duck down to avoid being hit.

"Boys certainly are the deuce," declared the engineer with a laugh; "they think we are fair game."

"I'll give them a little of their own game!" grinned Jim as he picked up a couple of stones on the seat opposite, and he leaned out of the window of the door, sending a stone at the group with accuracy and precision.

"Look at the guy!" they yelled; "paste him in the head."

To their surprise Jim did not duck back at their return volley but fended off a couple of the shots with his forearm, and one he caught with his right hand as though it were a baseball, and hurled it back with a snappy, short arm throw that caught the thrower squarely on the thigh.

"Hurrah for you, fellar!" yelled the crowd.

Jim acknowledged the salute with a graceful wave of his hand.

"Catching 'em Bill!" he yelled up at the driver.

"Gained half a block on 'em!" cried Bill with enthusiasm.

Jim could just make out a dark blur in the fog ahead where the pursued hack was galloping to some unknown destination. At the sight all the fierce excitement of the chase came over Jim. He must not let that Mexican escape this time. It meant everything to get a hold of him. He would recover his treasure belt, whose loss was not only a serious blow to his present plans, but an injury to his natural pride and confidence in himself. He could imagine his brother Tom saying:

"Ought to have had me along, Jim; you are too innocent to travel alone."

Hearing the voice of his comrade, Jim drew in his head.

"Catch a sight of the black pirate craft?" inquired the engineer.

"Dead ahead, and a smooth sea, sir," replied Jim touching his hat.

"Glad to be off the pebbles anyway, Captain," returned the engineer; "it may aid digestion, but it is doocid hard on old bones, like mine."

"I'm going upon deck with the pilot," said Jim. "I can't stay below here while that fellow is within hail."

"Natural feeling, Jim," agreed the engineer, "but you will have to have the Jehu up there slow down."

"Can't afford to lose the time," declared Jim. "I can reach the forward step and make it all right."

"Risky," said the engineer, "but that fact won't stop you."

He was correct, it did not, and the driver almost fell off his box in astonishment when he saw Jim's head at his elbow.

"Hey! what's this!" he yelled, as he clubbed his whip to strike. "Oh! it's you is it, Mister," he changed his tone when he saw who it was. "By thunder! I thought I was to be kilt."

"I'll sit in front here, Bill," said Jim genially. "I want to keep an eye open to see that that greaser don't give us the slip."

"He's there in that hack yet," assured the driver; "he hain't had a chance to jump out yit."

"They ain't pulling ahead are they?" inquired Jim, anxiously.

"Holding 'em level going down this hill," replied the driver. "My horse is a leetle heavy for a down grade, but you will see something different when we are going up hill or on the flat."

"I believe you," said Jim heartily; "that horse of yours is a good one."

"Paid five hundred for him, he ought to be," declared his owner proudly.

Inside the hack the engineer was making himself as comfortable as possible. His feet were upon the opposite seat, the green carriage robe was wrapped snugly around him and his head was dented back into the soft cushions. He was thoroughly enjoying the chase in his own way. The lurching of the vehicle did not disturb him, and he felt a certain pleasure in the freedom from any immediate responsibility. There was an excitement, too, in not knowing where the chase would carry. It was all a strange section of the city where they now were. He could see the ghostly fronts of long lines of houses, one not distinguishably different from another, but as similar as if they had been sawn from the same block of wood. The fog palliated many a monstrosity of wooden ornament, little balcony, or carved pinnacle.

If John Berwick was quiescent on the inside of the hack, Jim was on the *qui vive* on the outside. He had no idea of the direction in which they were going, but he was determined never to lose sight of that particular hack. At this moment they reached the bottom of a long hill. An eddy of air lifted the fog aside for an instant and Jim saw a head thrust out of the window of the hack.

"Geewillikins!" he exclaimed, wrathfully; "that isn't the greaser!"

Sure enough the head was not that belonging to the Mexican at all. It was a shaggy bearded face that leered back at Jim, and then he shouted some direction to the driver, and with a belligerent shake of his fist at Jim, jerked his head back.

"I guess that hunchback is in there all the same," cried the driver.

"He'd better be," growled Jim.

At the motion made by the bushy whiskered man, the driver of the first carriage in this active procession, turned his team at right angles into a street running east. "Bill" followed suit making a dangerous swerve, that almost overturned his vehicle, but it righted itself against the curb, and on the pursuit went. But Jim was beginning to be worried, for the big horse was tiring rapidly, while the mustangs seemed unflagging in their energy.

"How far have we gone?" asked Jim.

"About two miles, Boss," replied the driver.

"It won't be long till dusk," said Jim, "with this fog rolling in."

"I'll get back, what they have gained on us," declared Bill with conviction, "before they have gone another mile."

Jim noticed that this new turn was taking them into an apparently better section of the city, where there were really some fine-looking residences.

"They are making a stern chase of it, Jim," called Berwick, poking his head out of the window.

"We will catch them yet, Chief," declared Jim with outward confidence.

"Good boy!" replied the engineer. "I must say I like your spirit."

"How are you putting in the time down there, John?" queried Jim.

"Taking it easy," replied Berwick; "resting up in case I have to hustle a little later on."

"Wise man!" rejoined Jim; "just as well to save your energies. There will be something doing pretty soon or I miss my guess. We should overhaul them on the next hill."

"You look kind of damp, better get under cover, Jim," urged John Berwick. Indeed Jim did have a dampish look—his eyelashes and eyebrows were beaded with the moisture.

"No, I'm going to stay on deck until we overhaul those

pirates," he replied, "and it won't be long either."

However, it was somewhat longer than Jim thought. It seemed that the driver of the forward coupe was determined to make a clean getaway at this point for he laid on the whip with fierce determination.

CHAPTER XI

THE CHASE CONTINUED

After going a half a mile further, the leader in the race made another sharp turn, and a short distance ahead his goal was in sight, or it would have been had not the heavy fog prevailed. Of this, Jim was of course in nowise aware. Suddenly the hack ahead whirled and came to a stop. Two figures leaped out into the fog and started on the run.

Jim thrust a coin into the willing grasp of "Bill," and leaped to the ground closely followed from the cab by John Berwick, leaving the two drivers to themselves, and only a few yards apart. These worthies taking no further interest in the performance of their recent fares, engaged in a wordy altercation as to the rival merits of their steeds, and each had a different answer to the problem of "who won the race?" The outcome of this led to blows; as to the result, that belongs to another chronicle than mine. We are at present concerned with the race between Jim and the Mexican, with the chief and "Bushy Whiskers" as runners up.

Jim bounded after the fleeing Mexican and his comrade, with all the speed of his pent-up energy, and was overtaking him rapidly, when what looked like a high dark rampart showed indistinct through the fog a few rods ahead. Then the

Mexican bent low and darted out of sight, and his sturdy companion bounding high in the air disappeared.

Jim was thrown suddenly backward; as in mad pursuit, he dashed into an almost invisible fence of wire, steel colored, —which luckily was not barbed. The engineer who was a few paces behind, stopped in the nick of time, his outstretched hand easily breaking the force of his collision.

"Hurt, Jim?" he queried.

"Naw!" replied James. "Come on, John, let's see if you can jump like his whiskers."

"I'm no rat like that greaser," replied Berwick; "I can't crawl through, I've got to jump."

He showed himself something of an acrobat by the grace and agility with which he vaulted the six foot fence, and Jim went over with more power if less grace. Now they were in a quandary for directly before them was a wood of the tall and ghostly eucalyptus, into which the two fugitives had fled.

"We ought to have told our carriage to wait, Jim," said the chief engineer, with nonchalant humor. "This reminds me of two needles and a haystack."

"I've got their trail, Chief, come on before it gets too dark," ordered Jim, who had been casting around like a hound for a scent.

"You are the 'Boy Scout, or the Young Kit Carson,' for fair, James," cried Berwick, giving him a hearty slap of admiration between his broad shoulders.

Jim grinned but made no reply as he followed the trail into

the depth of the wood, which was made weird by the slender forms of the trees whose high tops were hidden by the low hanging mists that were as the breath of the huge ocean. The waters of the ocean not far away were slowly surging through the narrow pass of "The Golden Gate."

Then the hanging white strips of bark from the tall eucalyptus trees, added to the ghostly effect of the interior of the wood. James noticed none of these things for his attention was fixed on following the trail of his enemies. Here his long training in wood and plain craft stood him in good stead. It was his friend, Captain Graves, way back in Colorado, who had given him his first lessons in this difficult art and he could have had no better tutor than the captain, who had himself qualified in many a hard contest with the crafty Indian.

Now the Mexican was subtle, if not crafty, and the ordinary observer, even if he were as intelligent and quick as John Berwick, undoubtedly would have been entirely at sea in following the trail. Jim's keen senses, however, trained for such work, were not to be so easily baffled. The Mexican alone would have been exceedingly hard to have tracked, but his heavier footed comrade disturbed the fallen leaves or left a print in the red soil that betrayed the trail.

However, the pursuers were of necessity slowed down to a certain degree so that their chance of overtaking the two rascals grew slimmer every second. At that moment, however, their chase was given a new impetus. It came with a suddenness that was startling. From some distance ahead, it was difficult to tell how far, there came a furious chorus of yelps, barks and howls.

"Dogs!" cried Jim; "they have got our quarry treed!"

"Wild dogs, too!" said the engineer. "I've run across packs of them traveling in Mongolia. Ugly customers they are, too, unless you are good and ready for them."

At that instant there came the sharp report of half-a-dozen pistol shots, and the yelps were turned to howls of pain.

"Why didn't our friends in front ambush us and load us up with some of those lead pellets," remarked John Berwick thoughtfully.

"Perhaps they hadn't got to the place that suited them," said Jim, "or maybe they have orders from old Captain Broome to take us alive rather than dead. You know he is a man who likes to settle his own grudges, rather than by proxy."

"You must be something of a mind reader, James," remarked Berwick.

"I'm not that," declared Jim, "but I have had some dealing with Captain Bill Broome so I can judge."

Meanwhile the two friends were making straight for the noise of the fracas, and when they had gone about two hundred yards they were surprised by the dash of a big, gaunt, snarling yellow hound, who made a leap for Jim with teeth wide spread. Now James was unarmed, not his usual practice, but he was not in the habit of taking lunch at a restaurant armed to the teeth so that when this chase started he was not armed, else the venture would have come to an end long ago.

However, he did have his long, sharp-edged poniard with him. This he could carry inconspicuously in a belt around his waist. He slipped it from its sheath and met the charge of the hound squarely on his bent knee. He was bent back by the fury of the hound's rush, but he got in a thrust with a deadly precision that left the dog done for on the ground.

The engineer was not so lucky as Jim, he had no weapon of any kind and a small limb of a tree that he had hurriedly picked up proved no defense against the attack of a huge black brute, true of mongrel breed, but none the less ugly. He had knocked prostrate the engineer, who was not a large man, and was raving for his throat with cruel jaws, being held off for the moment only, by Berwick's clever use of the stick he had retained in his clutch when felled.

Jim was quick to see his friend's need. He dared not waste one single second, but with a low rush, he grappled with the brute, and by a sudden surge of his really great strength he thrust the beast to one side and for a moment they struggled fiercely on even terms, Jim's hand gripping the animal's throat, while the red, dripping jaws were striving to close on Jim's shoulder.

Exerting all his strength he managed to twist the beast off his balance and before it could recover had sent the death thrust home. The rest of the pack of smaller dogs evidently did not dare to come on and for a moment Jim rested panting, covered with sweat and blood.

"You certainly saved my neck that time, Jim," acknowledged John Berwick. "I guess it is hanging I'm reserved for."

"If you are ready we will move on; I'm afraid that trail will get cold," said Jim.

"I'm with you," declared the engineer, "but I rather hope that we will soon be out of these woods."

"Here's a little stream," remarked Jim, after they had gone a few yards, "guess I had better remove the signs of the late murder."

"You can see where those fellows crossed," remarked Berwick; "here is the mark of the big fellow's shoes."

"You have the making of a detective in you, John," said Jim with a perfectly sober face.

"Oh! I can detect all right, if it is thrust directly under my nose," agreed the engineer, with a smile.

"I don't see for the life of me how you keep so neat, Chief," remarked Jim, as he wrung out his stained handkerchief; "you look ready to enter into the best society, at a moment's notice." The engineer had taken off his brown hat and was smoothing his hair with a gentle stroke that Jim recognized was characteristic of him and this had provoked his remark about his friend's neatness.

"Hardly as bad as that, James," returned Berwick with a smile, "but I must admit that for some reason I never get very badly mussed in appearance no matter what the occasion may be."

Jim regarded his friend thoughtfully, carefully drying his hands meanwhile.

"I should like to wager a reasonable amount, Berwick, that you always don a dress suit for dinner," said Jim finally.

"Why, yes, I do," agreed the engineer, "whenever there is a chance. It makes you feel like a human being after the grease and grime of the engine room."

"Something in that," admitted Jim. "Well, let's hike."

CHAPTER XII

THE CASTLE

Jim's persistence was rewarded in a short time, when they came to the boundary of the wood. Here they found the trail very clearly marked, as in the old game of hare and hounds where the point of a new departure is marked by a bunch of cut paper. So in this case there were clear footprints, where the two rascals had cleared the fence and lighted on the damp earth on the other side.

"Where do you suppose they are heading for?" asked the engineer.

"The devil or the deep sea," replied Jim, humorously inclined.

"If they follow this direction, it will be the deep sea for certain," remarked Berwick, "for this trail is making straight for the bay, or I miss my guess."

"I bet anything that those two guys are planning to reach the *Sea Eagle*, and there will be a boat lying in some cove to take them out," said Jim decisively.

"Surely Captain Broome wouldn't have the gall to bring your

captured yacht into the bay right under the nose of the authorities," said the engineer.

"Huh!" grunted Jim; "that wouldn't be anything extraordinary for old Broome to do. He'd delight in it; and another thing, according to my idea the authorities and Captain William Broome ain't on such bad terms but what they can shut an eye to some of his performances. Besides it was his ship in the first instance," concluded Jim with a grin.

"A pirate don't have any title, anyhow," remarked the engineer.

"Maybe he does in San Francisco," remarked Jim with great simplicity.

At this Jim's chief engineer laughed heartily.

"That would be true doctrine enough for my native town of New York," he said.

"Well, howsumever, Captain Broome don't need any title. He keeps what he has and takes what he hasn't."

"You are an epigrammatist, Jim," said Berwick, smiling.

"Won't I ever outgrow it?" asked Jim anxiously.

"No, you will get worse as you become older," declared his friend.

"Gee, that's a bad outlook. Well, where there is life there is hope," replied Jim; "no use nosing this trail along, we have got the general direction and we want to get to the beach just as soon as we can so as to head those fellows off."

The two of them then started on a brisk trot and in a short time they heard the roar of the surf on the sand. But about a quarter of a mile from the beach they came to a halt, for a high fence barred their way.

"Hello, what does this mean?" inquired Jim with interest.

"It means we have come on someone's private estate," remarked the engineer, "and judging from the sharpness of these iron spikes, they are not at home to ordinary folks like us."

"I can just make out the house," remarked Jim, "and it looks like a big one."

There was the indistinct loom of the house through the fog; it appeared to be made of brick, with white trimmings and a huge chimney in the center clad with ivy. This was a good many years ago, and no remnant of this place remains to-day, for fire and earthquake wrought the ruin of this mansion, long before the catastrophe of 1906.

"Let's walk around this estate before it gets completely dark," said Jim, "which will be pretty soon now."

"You don't suppose that those two misguided pirates live here, do you?" questioned the engineer.

"Hardly," admitted Jim, "but they might be hiding in the yard."

"It would be tough work getting over," said the engineer, "especially with what is coming from the direction of the house." Jim looked and pulled his friend down behind the parapet of stone in which the iron fence was set.

"Perhaps it won't see us," said Jim in a low voice. But they were a wee bit too late to escape detection. Between the shrubbery there came at a menacing lope, a huge, yellow-white, bloodhound, with hanging dew laps, and following him a great Dane whose velvety black form held a real ferocity. They leaped high with their forefeet against the iron fence, striving frantically to reach the two men on the other side.

"They are more dangerous than the mountain lion, those dogs," said Berwick.

"I'm very glad to be on this side of the fence," admitted Jim. "We wouldn't stand much show without our guns."

"I thought you ate them alive," laughed John Berwick, referring to the incident in the wood.

"It was to keep you from being eaten up yourself," grinned Jim. "Say, Chief, let's move out of range, or these beasts will rouse the whole country."

"All right, Captain," agreed Berwick, using Jim's sea title, and as they were rather at sea, it was quite appropriate. They reached a large rock that stood out on the plain away from the house, and sat down on it, until the noise of the baying had ceased.

"Did you think to fetch a lunch with you on this festive occasion, James?" inquired Berwick.

"Bah Jove, old chap," replied James, "we left in such haste that it slipped my mind, don't yer know."

"I wish your mind hadn't been so slippery," remarked the engineer. "If you could only have had presence of mind enough to have brought an olive or two."

"I tell you, Chief," said Jim, airily, "I'll have the dinner ready by the time you get your dress suit. But coming down to the plain English of it, I'm starved. Think of the exercise we have had since leaving the restaurant to join our friend on the sidewalk."

"A man who would put you to all that trouble to speak to him is no gentleman," declared John Berwick whimsically.

"He deserves to be hung," said Jim savagely; "anyone who would impose on a trustful nature like yours and make you run over twenty miles of landscape! But cheer up, John, I have a hunch that we will strike a pay streak of grub yet. Let's take one more scout around that mysterious castle yonder and then we will make a bee line for the nearest lunch counter."

"Any time you give the word."

"Well, I suppose that 'all's quiet along the Potomac,' so let's move."

"Agreed, James," said the engineer.

Then the two friends slipped through the soft darkness of the night and fog until they reached the iron rampart of the fence and went past the great gates. There was a gilt monogram on either side and in the center, but these things did not interest them. Then they went on to the south part of the grounds.

"See that, John!" said Jim in a low voice.

"A light in the tower," replied his friend; "now it's gone out again."

They stood watching with breathless interest. There are lights and lights. Some are the mere commonplace of domestic peace set on a round table in a cozy room with children intent on the Frontier Boys. Then there is the weird light of a lantern moving unevenly across a field, or revolving along a hidden lane, and there is something of the dramatic in its yellow flame. Finally there is the light that shines under strange circumstances or peculiar surroundings that has a mystery of its own, a beacon of danger, or of sudden death.

"It is again on this side, only higher up," announced Jim; "somebody going up those stairs, that's what it is."

In a few moments the powerful lamp illuminated an upper room and they saw the interior distinctly. But what fastened their attention was the sight of a head that showed just above the sill of the windows. It must be the head of a child to reach no higher. But what would a child be doing up in that lonely tower. Jim gripped his companion's arm.

"It's that infernal Mexican, Berwick!" he whispered.

"No other!" said his friend. "And that light is a signal."

"Can't be seen far even if the fog is thinner," objected Jim.

"Broome is close in," said the engineer decisively.

"It may be to serve as a guide for some party coming over the lonely moor," said Jim with much shrewdness.

"Go to the head of the class, James," remarked Berwick; "that's a sound guess for a fact."

"Guess nothing," retorted Jim; "that's a deduction as they say in the school books. What in the deuce is that up there now!"

A canine head was outlined in an open window and then the big hound gave tongue that went far into the night. His senses told him that an enemy was lurking near.

"My! what a mark for a shot!" whispered Jim.

Then they heard a sharp command in Spanish and both the dog and the Mexican disappeared from view.

"We had better move along, Jim," said the engineer, "or we will be on the hot end of a chase ourselves." Without a word Jim started, but he would not run far.

CHAPTER XIII

THE MAN IN THE GULLY

The two friends disappeared in the fog, in a southerly direction from the house and after going for about a quarter of a mile, Jim called a sudden halt.

"Hold on, John," he said, "there is something coming our way."

"I don't hear anything," replied Berwick. "What does it sound like?"

"It's a vehicle of some kind," declared Jim.

"Now I hear it," admitted the engineer, "and I reckon that it is a carriage of some kind."

"This is as good a place as any," remarked Jim. "It's lucky there is a fog because there is no cover to get behind."

"Coming direct our way," said the engineer, as the thud of horses' feet could be heard distinctly, and the low roll of wheels over the ground.

The two comrades moved quickly to one side, and they saw

emerge from the fog a high-stepping team drawing a closed carriage. The horses shied at what they saw at the side of the way, but the coachman pulled them quickly to their course and drove rapidly on. It was impossible to get even a glimpse of the occupants of the carriage.

"Me lord Duke," said Jim, "going to his ancestral castle."

"That's surely where he is bound for," declared the engineer.

"There goes the gate," cried Jim, as the sound of the iron closing came to his ears.

"The plot thickens," remarked the engineer; "that wasn't an ordinary turnout by any means."

"We will investigate this business before morning," determined Jim, "but there is nothing gained by rushing,—better let things settle. What do you say, John, to getting something to eat?"

"I'm with you there," agreed Berwick. "I may have been hungrier in my life before, but I can't remember."

"No Russian Duke this time to help you out, eh?" queried Jim.

"Don't mention that," cried the engineer; "I'm in no need of an appetiser."

If you have read "Frontier Boys in The Sierras," you will recall the chief engineer's account of his experience while traveling from St. Petersburg to the frontier, when he appropriated the Grand Duke's hamper while his Highness was wrapped in the deep stupor of sleep. He had told it with much nerve and vivacity, and Jim could recollect very clearly the scene in the warm engine-room of the *Sea Eagle*, with the stormy rain sweeping the decks outside, and the good old crowd of Juarez, and the boys, listening to the engineer.

"I have a hunch that we are going to get something to eat soon," remarked Jim encouragingly.

"Shall we strike the trail back to the city, and return in the small wee hours to call on our friends in the castle?" asked Berwick.

"No need of that," replied Jim; "I am sure we can find a place to eat down by the beach."

They had a little difficulty in finding a break in the cliffs that walled the water front, but finally they discovered a cleft in the solid rock and they were able to make a steep descent over broken bowlders. They were halfway down when Jim stopped so abruptly that the engineer stumbled against him.

"See that man sitting against that rock," he whispered; "he looks as if he were asleep."

"Maybe drunk," remarked John Berwick.

"Or a sentinel for the castle," put in Jim.

He felt around at his feet until he picked up a suitable rock, then closely followed by the engineer, he approached cautiously the figure against the rock, then Jim deliberately went up and looked into the man's face.

"He's dead," said Jim in a quiet voice. "I've seen too many like him not to know."

"Who do you suppose got him," queried the engineer.

"Those friends of ours on the hill, no doubt," said Jim. "Yes, it's their work," he declared, as he ran his hand along under the man's coat; "stabbed in the back." The unfortunate fell heavily against Jim's shoulder and one of his legs straightened out convulsively.

"You have a pretty fair quality of nerve, my friend," remarked the engineer in cool admiration.

"Strike a light, John," said Jim, "and see if we can get a line on this poor fellow."

The engineer drew a pretty trinket of a match box from his upper vest pocket and struck a match near the face. There was such a direct living look in the man's half-closed eyes, that the engineer dropped the match with an involuntary expression of surprise and shock.

"What's the matter with you, John?" asked Jim with a touch of sharpness in his voice. The engineer was a man of usual nonchalant nerve, whose bravery had always seemed a by-product of his nature and not due to an effort of the will, which gave point to Jim's question.

"I am getting shaky in my old age, Captain," replied the engineer.

"No danger of that," replied Jim.

Again a match was lit and this time Berwick held the flame close to the dead man's face. They saw that he was not over forty years of age, with a heavy square jaw, a full straw colored mustache, and hazel eyes. He wore a light gray fedora hat and his suit was also of gray, loosely worn. He was squarely built, and slightly below the middle height. There was absolutely nothing to indicate his business, or his station in life. Whatever possessions he may have had on him had been taken.

"What was the reason for this, John?" questioned Jim, as he gently laid the dead man back against the rock.

"Robbery?" suggested Berwick.

"They are none too good," replied Jim, "as I can testify from personal experience. But I reckon that there is more back of this than that.

"Now I may be mistaken, but in my opinion this man was a United States detective and he was hot on the trail of this gang of pirates and smugglers. I used to know a number of these fellows in New York and there is something about them that marks them to my mind."

"I bet you have hit it right," said Jim, "but why did they not hide the body?"

"Possibly they are so safe in this section that they don't take the trouble to cover up their crime," remarked the engineer tentatively.

"Or they may be intending to come back to-night and dispose of the body," said Jim.

"That's more apt to be it," agreed the engineer.

"It might be a good scheme to lie in wait for a while, and see if any of these hounds come back on their trail," suggested Jim.

Wyn Roosevelt

The engineer of the *Sea Eagle* who was at present out of his element, drew a deep sigh and likewise drew up his belt a couple of holes, which was his alternative for a meal, that he seemed fated to go without. The unsympathetic Jim grinned at his comrade in arms.

"I tell you, Chief," he said, "we will catch one of these grand rascals and cook him a la cannibal."

"I would be most happy to," replied the engineer suavely and savagely.

"We will move down the ravine a ways," ordered Jim.

"My idea was that they would come down from the top of the cliff," said the engineer with cool criticism.

"That was my idea, too," said Jim cheerfully; "then we might follow them without too much chance of being caught ourselves."

"You are certainly long on strategy, James," remarked the engineer.

"Hello, Berwick," exclaimed Jim; "there is a light ahead."

Sure enough on the beach at the mouth of the ravine shone the yellow light from a small square window. They crept up carefully to the place. It was rather a curious affair. It was simply two old street cars joined together by a wooden vestibule; one was used as a sleeping room the other was a tiny beach eating place. Jim looked in cautiously through the window and his eyes widened and his hand went involuntarily to where his revolver usually hung. He remained there a full half minute taking in the scene within while the engineer stood a little ways back in apparent indifference, but he was carefully taking in the whole situation. A short distance away the waters of the bay were lapping through the darkness onto the beach.

He noticed that there were a number of heavy tracks going towards the door of the odd little restaurant, and they were quite recent. He listened intently to hear, if possible, who might be inside, but while he could distinguish voices, there were only a few noncommittal sounds. He wondered what the captain found so interesting, but just then there came a scuffling of chairs on the floor within and the sound of guttural voices. Jim drew back suddenly, and in evident alarm. The door was slowly opened and a heavy figure dressed in sailor garb lurched out into the darkness followed by a stealthy form.

CHAPTER XIV

THE VISITOR

"I wonder what mischief the old man is chawing on?" It was the forward deck of the *Sea Eagle*, and the speaker, Old Pete, the sailor, of unsavory memory. "He's been as savage as a bear with a sore head two days past, and that means he's brewing some sort of devilment."

"Maybe he's watching to trail some craft going out with a rich cargo," said Jack Cales, of likewise deleterious recollection, who was seated on the forward hatch, opposite the ancient mariner who was himself resting on a coil of rope.

"I dunno about that," said Pete, puffing meditatively on his black, stunted pipe; "according to my notion it's something ashore. Old Hunch was aboard airly this mornin', and that greaser is a sure sign of trouble. Reminds me of a croaking black raven. I'd like to wring his wry neck for him. He ain't fit to associate with respectable pirates like us."

"I don't see why the cap'n sets such store by him, anyhow," protested Jack Cales.

"It's an unhung gang of bloody cutthroats the old man's got ashore," remarked Old Pete. "I wouldn't want any trafficking with them."

There was something amusing in this feud between the rascals on ship and ashore, something like the rivalry between the navy and army.

"Shut your jaw," said Cales peremptorily; "here comes the cap'n now."

To the earlier readers of "The Frontier Boys," he is a familiar figure but he is well worth introducing to those who are meeting him for the first time. Captain William Broome, familiarly known as Bill, or the old man, was a remarkable person. There was a strange softness in Captain Broome's tread, like that of the padded panther, as he came forward along the main deck. He appeared like a man always ready to get a death hold upon a nearby enemy, both wary and using unceasing watchfulness. This was evident in the crouching gait of his powerful figure. His arms had the loose forward swing of a gorilla's, indicative of enormous strength.

"That man a pirate!" you exclaim at the first glance. One who carried the blackest name along the coasts of the two American continents as a wrecker and smuggler; who in the days before the Civil War had brought cargoes of slaves from Africa, and who had enjoyed more marvelous escapes than any man in the history of piracy, with the exception of Black Jack Morgan? "Impossible!" you say. "Why, that man is nothing but an old farmer," you cry in disappointment. "He ought to be peddling vegetables in a market!" But just wait.

True enough, Skipper Broome had come from a long line of New England farmers, hard, close-fisted, close-mouthed men. Young Broome had broken away from the farm, and followed his bent for seafaring, but to the end of his rope, and his days, he kept his farmer-like appearance, and he affected many of the traits of the yeoman, which he found to be, on more than one occasion, a most useful disguise.

Let's take a look at him, as he comes along the deck of the *Sea Eagle*. The heavy winter cap, which he wore in season and out of season, pulled well down on his grizzled head, gave him a most Reuben-like appearance. Corduroy pants are thrust into heavy cowhide boots. The deadly gray eyes, no softer than granite, have become red-rimmed from spasms of fury and rendered hard by many scenes of coldly-calculated cruelty.

"Yaw two gents enjying the balmy air for'ard, on your bloomin' pleasure yacht?" inquired Captain William Broome, who had a turn for broad sarcasm.

"Jus' smokin' a few peaceful pipes, sir," replied Pete, who was allowed a certain amount of leeway with his master, as he had been with him in the African trade, and as boys in New England, they had lived on nearby farms.

"This ain't no time for peaceful meditation," said the captain; "you git aft and keep a sharp eye abeam, and if you see any boat creepin' through the fog, even if it's an innercent looking fishin' boat, you report it to the mate."

"Aye, aye, sir," replied Pete as he stowed his pipe in his capacious pocket, and maneuvering a safe distance from the captain's foot, went on his mission. Then Broome spit carefully around on the deck.

"Here, Cales, you loafer, clean this yere deck up," he growled.

Thus, having made himself pleasant to all hands, he went forward and, leaning heavily on the rail, looked shoreward as if expecting a messenger of some kind. It was impossible to tell the exact position of the *Sea Eagle* in the immense bay of San Francisco. One thing was certain, that it was not near the shore where the castle stood on the cliff, for the current and the depth of water made it impossible to anchor. However, it was near some shore, for the sound of the surf could be heard distinctly. Five minutes passed and then the captain raised himself up with a grunt of satisfaction. A long trim boat had slipped quietly from the enveloping fog into the quiet circle of the sea around the yacht.

The oars were not muffled but they made as little noise as though they were. It was rowed by four men, quite evidently foreigners; brown men, two with rings in their ears, and the others were splendidly built fellows, who rowed as easily as they breathed. These latter were Hawaiians, who are as native to the sea and its ways as the cowboys to their own western plains. They were part of the mixed crew which the old pirate had got together for reasons of his own. The said reasons being that such a crew could not very well combine to mutiny or to rob him of his ill-gotten wealth.

In the stern of the ship's cutter was an entirely different looking man from the kind with whom Captain Broome was generally associated. If the man had been a priest or a parson his presence in such company would have been no more surprising. He had the appearance of a well-dressed gentleman, probably a professional man of some kind. His features were good and his dress impeccable.

Against the chill fog he wore a dark overcoat, with silk facings, and a black derby hat. At his feet, on the bottom of the boat, was a long black leather bag, somewhat like those which physicians carry. Yet he was not a doctor, for it was generally the enemies of Captain Broome who needed the services of a physician.

The boat glided gently by the perforated platform of the gangway and was held firmly by the oarsmen, while the stranger stepped with a quick, precise step from the small boat. The captain was on hand and greeted him with a certain awkward courtesy, for politeness was not in his line.

"Glad to see yer, Mr. Reynolds," he said, giving him a grip from his horny hand; "hope you didn't get damp from the fog, crossin'."

"It's nothing, Captain," replied the man-crisply, an amused sneer hidden under his mustache; "fog is my element. It agrees perfectly with my delicate health."

"I'm relieved to hear it," remarked Captain Broome gently. "Come up to my cabin, sir, and I'll give you a drink of something that will clear the fog for you."

The professional gentleman, from the city, followed his sinister host up the gangway and into his cabin, while the boat pushed away from the side of the yacht, bowed softly to the gentle swell of the sea. It was like a carriage that is waiting for the return trip. The two Hawaiians were laughing and joking in characteristic good humor, which is entirely different from the boisterous jollity of the darkies.

They were having sport by laughing at their passenger. His neatness of demeanor and style of dress seemed to furnish them with much amusement. With their quickness for giving nicknames, they called him, "Mr. Blackbag," and the captain was known to them as Roaring Bull. They were very apt, as all Hawaiians are, to see the defects of character and weak points of those white people who came under their observation.

Meanwhile the captain and his guest sat in the latter's cabin, discussing matters that will soon concern us gravely. This cabin, as perhaps the reader remembers, was a good sized room. A large table of cherry wood was against one side, with a few maps and books on it. A broad bunk was curtained off with red draperies. There was a scarred sea chest against the opposite wall, fastened by a heavy padlock. On this the captain was firmly seated.

To complete the description I may say that the room was paneled in white, and contrary to what you might expect, the cabin was absolutely neat. Broome's visitor had turned the swivel chair halfway from the desk, and was directly facing the hard-faced captain, who had taken off his heavy cap, showing his bald and polished dome of thought that glowed red under the light of the big, swinging, brass lamp. The shuttered window was closed against the dim daylight outside. This was a secret conclave and with good reason. Upon the table at Mr. Reynold's elbow the black satchel was opened. Its contents at first glance were not startling. But wait!

CHAPTER XV

THE LAWYER AND THE PIRATE

The contrast between the two men as they sat facing each other was really dramatic; the rough hewn captain, in his countrified garb, and the city man correct in dress and quiet in manner; but as to which was the most dangerous villain it would be hard to decide off hand.

Mr. William Howard Reynolds was primarily a lawyer, but he was likewise agent and adviser for several organizations whose aims were not high but very direct. He had been of aid to Captain Broome several times before, had smoothed over several unfortunate affairs with the local authorities on behalf of his client and had been liberally rewarded for so doing. Where finesse and criminal adroitness were concerned he was of the greatest use to the captain of the *Sea Eagle*.

It was doubtful if he had ever been engaged in a more nefarious scheme than he had in hand upon this particular occasion. As he sits facing the captain with the light slanting across his face let us take a square look at this man, so that we shall be able to recognize him if we should chance to meet him again.

As has been said he was well attired, and with his light weight overcoat off, he is seen to be dressed in a dark cut-a-way coat with a white vest according to the custom of that remote time. He wore upon the forefinger of his left hand a peculiar serpent ring, whose ruby eyes seemed really to glow in the light. He used this ring finger on occasion to drive home a convincing argument.

His own dark, close set eyes always followed the line of this gesture with telling effect. It was these eyes together with a cruel mouth, at one corner of which lurked a treacherous sneer, that showed the true character of the individual, for aside from these two features his face was not an unpleasant one. The forehead was high and well developed, the chin square and masculine. The wiry, but carefully brushed hair was already becoming gray around the temples. So much for Mr. William H. Reynolds, so far as his mental and physical photograph goes.

"Well, Captain Broome," he said, leaning forward with the weight of his hands upon the arms of the chair, "what is your scheme in this business?"

"I haven't any, Mr. Reynolds," replied the captain mildly; "you know that I am a plain man, just a simple, seafaring old codger and am greatly afeared of being shanghaied ashore by some of the villains that reside there."

The lawyer threw back his head and laughed harshly.

"I've noticed that it is the plain, farmer looking chap, that's the deepest often," he said, "but I know that you didn't invite me out to your yacht for afternoon tea. Let's get down to business."

"As I said, I ain't got a scheme, but I'll give you the facts and let you hatch the scheme." There was an unconscious contempt in the captain's voice, which the keen lawyer was quick to recognize, but did not care to resent. His client was too valuable to risk a breach with, so he merely tightened his jaws, and waited for the captain to begin.

At this juncture in the interview the captain got up quickly from the locker on which he had been seated. The motion was so sudden and menacing that the lawyer plunged his hand into the black bag on the table. Broome, if he noticed this action, gave no sign but crouched noiselessly to the door, opened it suddenly and rushed out upon the deck.

There was the sound of a low growl as of an uncaged animal, then a scuffling sound followed by a thud. In a moment the old pirate returned to his cabin, shut the door, and sat down as if nothing had happened, as indeed was the fact according to his idea of things. Meanwhile Cales, the sailor, who chanced to be cleaning the deck not far from the captain's cabin, picked himself up from the scuppers, whence he had been flung by Broome. He was bleeding and dazed, but not so dazed but what he could heap maledictions upon the head of his superior officer. Even in his wrath, however, he did not dare to speak above a hoarse whisper. The lawyer surmised what had happened but he made no comment as his genial client sat himself down again upon the sea chest.

"These are the facts, Mr. Reynolds, and I'll be brief because it is my nature." The captain leaned forward heavily on his knees, and spoke in harsh confidence to his attorney, or rather agent, who listened intently, but with an inscrutable face. "There's a rich Mexican with a Spanish name, Senor da Cordova, over in the city right now and he has been trying to make a dicker with me to get hold of my yacht. He's interested in helping those Cuban niggers who are fighting the Spaniards and he thinks this yere boat might come in handy in the business, and she would, too; there's nothing faster sailing these waters anyhow."

"He's coming a long ways around to get his cruiser," remarked the lawyer coolly.

"The other side is watched, and it ain't easy to pick up the right kind of craft anyway, without payin' a ransom, and this old Dick wants to drive a hard bargain, says it is a good cause and all that, but I ain't got no interest in those Cuban niggers."

"I follow you," said the lawyer, "but that isn't what you wanted me to help with."

He knew his client thoroughly.

"You're right it ain't," replied the captain with emphasis; "I made the contract to carry the shooting irons and we are loaded ready to sail, but the Senor's got a gal."

The lawyer looked keenly at his client.

"It's a case of kidnaping, then," remarked the lawyer with as much unconcern as if referring to an attack of measles.

"Yer have the right idea, Mr. Reynold's," said the candid mariner; "the gal's daddy sets a heap of store by her, and he'll pay something handsome to git her back, more than he would for this steam yacht of mine, twice over."

"Tell me how the land lies, Captain, then I'll give you my terms."

Captain Broome speaking in a low, growling voice, gave him the necessary details, and then with his bushy eyebrows knitted together he watched the other man with grim intentness. Mr. William H. Reynolds sat for some time with his head thrown back and half-closed eyes, gazing upward at the ceiling, and then he began to whistle softly with a slight hissing sound.

"It's the devil in him getting up steam," mused Broome; "he sees his way through all right."

Indeed he did, but he did not inform his valued client that he was well acquainted with the agent of the Cuban insurgents, who had come West to meet the Senor da Cordova, for he had no intention of belittling the difficulty of the task assigned him.

"How much?" inquired Captain Broome, in a noncommittal voice. These two wasted no time on formalities, they had been in too many transactions for that. By way of reply, the lawyer held up five fingers. Immediately the Yankee master put up three and a half by doubling his little finger, but the attorney remained firm.

"You'll get ten thousand out of this, you old reprobate," he said frankly, "and I take the risk. Take it or leave it, I've got some other matters to attend to immediately."

The captain grunted, he hated to pay, especially without a long bargaining, but he knew his friend well enough to realize that it was a waste of valuable time, and that one might just as well try to bargain with a graven image. Slowly he drew out a leather pouch from his capacious pants' pocket and opening it placed—How many twenty dollar gold pieces, Reader, to make five hundred dollars? Well, Tom, what is it? "Fifteen." You Johnny? "Twenty-five." Quite right.

They made a brave sight piled up in the light upon the table, but they did not stay in evidence very long for after noting each one carefully, he put it in the black bag, until they were all properly shepherded.

"Would you like to have this business finished to-day, Captain?" inquired the lawyer.

"You're right, I would," said Broome with emphasis.

"Make it a thousand, and I'll guarantee to do it," replied the lawyer. The captain's jaw fell.

"It is worth it, for the risk is double," returned the lawyer.

"I haven't anything like it with me," declared the captain. "I'm no gold mine."

"Give me your note then," said Reynolds, "payable in fifteen days."

"I tell you what I will do, Mr. Reynolds, I'll make it for three hundred; and more I can't do."

"Agreed," said the lawyer.

"Have a drink on it," urged the captain, hospitably, and feeling fairly well satisfied with his bargain.

"No time for that," replied the lawyer abruptly; "you'll be at the castle not later than ten and I'll make my part of the contract good. Tell those niggers of yours to dig in and row some going back."

The captain evidently gave them sound instructions, because they made record time, cutting through the fog at a slashing gait.

CHAPTER XVI

AN ODD RESTAURANT

Let us now return to our friends, Captain James Darlington and Chief Engineer John Berwick, of the good yacht, *Sea Eagle*, the latter now in the bad hands of Pirate William Broome. We left them crouching in the fog outside the car restaurant on the beach. Two men had come out into the fog. The first a big sailor as was evident by his gait, as well as his costume, and the man who followed in his wake was of a slinking type, and may have been a beachcomber. Jim could not make up his mind whether these two were members of the pirate crowd or not.

The two friends watched them until they merged into the darkness and fog, going towards the water and not in the direction of the castle. For one moment Jim got the idea that the smaller man meant mischief towards the big sailor, but he did not attempt to follow the pair for there was other fish for them to fry that night. After a minute's wait the engineer made a move as if to go towards the door of the queer little restaurant, but his comrade laid a restraining hand on his arm. Jim had learned due caution from his past experience with the Indians and treacherous border men, and for all he knew these two men might return after a short time, and make trouble for them. Ten minutes passed in perfect silence though the engineer began to feel extremely restive from hunger. Finally Jim rose to his feet.

"I reckon we will board this car, Pardner," he determined, "if you happen to have the fare."

"They've got the fare inside there," replied the engineer sententiously, "that I want."

Jim laughed, and then taking another look through the window to assure himself that no one else was inside, he opened the door and followed by his friend went in. It was a quaint looking place, lighted by a big ship's lamp in the center of the ceiling, that shed warmth as well as light. It had been a really large and spacious car, and there was plenty of room for the long, clean lunch counter, which was adorned with several clusters of condiments, salt and pepper shakers, and a heavy china sugar bowl. These surrounded a tall red ketchup bottle and a black sauce bottle.

There were likewise two small tables with several stools around them. At the far end of the car on either side of the heavily curtained portion, were two stained glass windows, one blue, and the other red. Both had the same design, that of a knight in full armor on a prancing horse, and a long lance at half cock, as it were.

"Vell, poys, vat you vant, eh?" questioned the short, fat German, in his white cap and apron, from behind the lunch counter. It was clear that he was not favorably impressed with these new customers, who were muddy, wet and bedraggled, from their long chase of the afternoon and evening. But do not make a mistake; it was not their character, which Fritz Scheff viewed askance; they might be cutthroats and villains of the deepest dye, and it would not worry him any in the least. But could they pay? that was the question.

John Berwick grasped the situation with sufficient clearness.

"What do we want, Old Sport?" he replied, airily; "every-thing you've got on the bill of fare. Here's a bill for a beginner." And the engineer threw a five dollar currency certificate on the clean wood counter.

The German's little, black eyes opened as wide as was possible, which was not saying much; he was not used to such lavishness on the part of customers. However, he was cautious, for such was his nature. He held up the bill to the light and then gave it a slight tug. This nettled Jim, who did not sympathize with his friend's extravagance at times.

"Donner and Blitzen mein freund," roared Jim, who used such language as came to his hand; "you old counterfeit. Get busy, we're hungry. And, another thing, you can stow that bill my friend gave you, but you've got to give him back what's coming to him."

"Which will be mighty little," said Berwick humorously, "because my appetite is growing some."

The proprietor's big red neck grew choleric under Jim's remark, but by a quick transformation he swallowed his wrath, and became a smiling and complacent host.

"Anydings you vants shentlemen is yours. Just give me de order."

He handed each of them a rather soiled menu in a frame and the two gaunt travelers regarded the list with a moment's deep interest.

"A Hamburg steak to start with," said the engineer, "and three fried eggs on the side not to mention some black coffee and hashed brown potatoes."

"The same here, friend," remarked Jim, "only put me down for two eggs."

"Bless me! what a delicate appetite, James!" exclaimed Berwick.

"I'm looking to something else, John!" replied Jim.

"Wise lad," remarked the engineer, "but do you know, as I can't have my dress suit on this auspicious occasion—"

"You mean suspicious," cut in Jim with a grin.

"Never mind that now," continued the engineer; "what I was going to say was that a plain—"

"High neck," interrupted Jim.

"Any old neck wash would be truly acceptable," concluded the engineer.

The proprietor heard and heeded.

"Eh, Anna, come here," he cried in stentorian German. There was a gentle shuffling sound and a creaking of a board from the direction of the other car or room and a large figure appeared in the curtained doorway.

"What is it you want, my Fritz?" questioned the placid and housewifely Anna, taking in the newcomers with a quiet gaze.

"The shentlemen of honorable wealth, Frau Scheff, would like to wash their esteemed countenances," he explained with ironical deference.

"Ach! that is good," said Mrs. Scheff with a fat good-natured smile; "trouble yourselves to come with me."

"By the time you shentlemans are washed and improved, the supper will be ready," said the proprietor.

The engineer was greatly amused by this stout German couple and showed it by a slight smile, but Jim who always had a native respect for decent and kindly people no matter who they were, had no intention of joining his friend in any humorous byplay in regard to the stout house frau.

She led them through the short passageway into the other room. One end was curtained off for the bedroom, with snowy white curtains tied back with pink ribbons.

Everything about the two little rooms was marvelously clean and neat. There was a big round globe lamp on a black oak table, ornamented with the quaint carvings of the Fatherland, on the standard. Nearby was a capacious rocking chair where the good frau had been sitting, and her knitting was on the table. On a cushion in front of the chair was a huge gray striped cat, comfortably curled and sound asleep. Jim who loved all animals could not resist stroking it and then gave its ears a twitch which made his catship raise his big head and open his mouth in that silent feline protest, which is so amusing.

"Ah, the Kaiser Fritz is a very spoiled cat. Is it not so liebchen?" and she lifted him bodily from his comfortable cushion. But the Kaiser was decidedly peeved by all this attention and showed it very plainly.

"Ach! you are a tiger! a French tiger! you deserve not the

good name of Fritz!" and with a temper as quick as her kindness, she threw him into the chair.

"The Kaiser Fritz is a fine animal, Frau Scheff," said Jim pleasantly; "I should like to own him."

"He eats as much as two kinder," said the frau with a sigh, "and he is not so grateful. Now you two gentlemen make yourselves welcome. Here are plenty towels."

Jim and the engineer thanked her, the former briefly, the latter with a pleasing grace that he could use when he so wished. But it was to be noted that while she surveyed John Berwick with a careful and noncommittal eye, she regarded Jim with a simple kindness that fairly beamed, which is not insinuating that the chief engineer of the *Sea Eagle* was a rascal but that he did not have the straightforward sincerity characteristic of Jim.

There were indeed towels enough hanging on the rack by the washstand, which with its drapings of white and blue was so dainty, that Jim regarded it as much too fine for mere washing.

"Look at this blue and white china washbowl and pitcher, Jim," remarked Berwick in a casual tone. "It is really beautiful. It is made in a town, in southern Germany, where I once spent a couple of months."

"Seems to me you have been everywhere on this created earth, John, and say," continued Jim, "see that mountain of a feather bed covered with the snow of the coverlet. You know that they make those in southern France where once I spent some months." The chief engineer grinned.

CHAPTER XVII

THE GOOD FRAU

After a thorough wash, the two compatriots felt very much refreshed, and looked less like street urchins or sea urchins, and more like themselves. Only one thing troubled the chief engineer, as he rubbed his hand reflectively over his chin and face.

"I would feel quite respectable now if I only had a clean shave. You know for a fact, Jim, that I can think much more clearly when my face is smooth. But that is something which you don't have to bother about, Jim, no reflection on your years, my lad," he concluded, with a smile.

"Better not be," replied Jim gruffly, coloring up, for be it known that James was sensitive on the point of being young. Funny thing, boy nature, anyway. John Berwick opened his eyes at Jim's tone, and then a quizzical look came into his face. There was no denying that Berwick had at times a vicious temper, but he was always good-natured where Jim was concerned, and never resented the latter's occasional flare of temper, which was greatly to his credit.

"You'll feel all right, Captain," he said gravely, "when you get your emptiness lined with beefsteak."

"I'm a chump to flare up for nothing, Chief," deplored Jim; "next time I do it give me a swift push into the alley." The engineer only shook his head good-humoredly, while he was giving his brown mustache a final twist before the glass; Jim was looking with interest at a photograph of a lad upon the wall. A well set up boy, with a grave, straightforward look.

"That is my Fritz," said a voice behind him. It was Frau Scheff. "He has been away from home now two years. His father was very strict with him and he love the sea, so he go away from home in some ship. He would be about your age, my lad, but not so tall. Perhaps some time you see him, and tell him, please, his mother break her heart to see him." Her voice trembled, and for a moment she pressed her hands against her eyes. Jim had a deep-seated aversion to any show of emotion, but this simple yearning in a mother's voice affected him deeply. His eyes filled with moisture for a moment.

"I promise you to keep your son in mind, Frau Scheff," he said in a quiet voice, "and it may not be at all impossible that I should some day meet him. Was there any certain mark by which I might recognize him?"

"Fritz had a scar about an inch long over his left eye, which he got when he was a little fellow," said the mother, "but ach! why do I make you to feel sorry with my troubles. Come! by this time my husband has your supper done." She regarded Jim with a benevolent smile and led the way through the narrow passage into the little restaurant. The savory smell of cooking greeted the hungry outcasts as they entered the car restaurant.

"Shentlemans, your repast is served." He waved his hand towards one of the little tables, which had on it a spotless white tablecloth, and the necessary implements for attacking the grub.

"Ah! it looks very good, Herr Scheff," said John Berwick, who could be very gracious when he wished. "Your name should be chef; you deserve it, my friend."

The German made a short bow and his round face crinkled into a smile.

"It is enough that you are pleased, honorable sir," he said.

"Ach, Fritz!" exclaimed his wife, "why do you give these friends of ourselves such knives and forks? I will get some of our own."

"Now don't you bother, Mrs. Scheff," said Jim; "these will do all right for us."

"Ach! no! no!" she exclaimed, shaking her head; "they will not do. The sailors bite the forks as though they eat them. I go get our own."

And she did. They were of heavy silver, with a quaint monogram on the handles of the forks. No doubt heirlooms of several generations back. Without more ado the two friends began with hearty appetites on the two portions of steaks, the delicately browned potatoes, and the eggs. Everything had a delicious taste, for, aside from their hunger, the meal was excellently cooked.

"I will make the coffee, Fritz," said his wife, "and how would you like some German pancake?"

"We would like nothing better," agreed the engineer.

"I'm good for any kind of a pancake," said Jim heartily, and he was not exaggerating, either.

How good that coffee did smell, and it tasted equal to its aroma. As for the big, flat, German pancakes, with their coating of powdered sugar and side dishes of apple sauce, pleasantly tart with sliced lemon,—well, Jim always had the tantalizing memory of them when in other days he was furiously hungry, which latter he was destined to be on more than one occasion. Jim, nevertheless, had not forgotten the business in hand, even while eating.

"Herr Scheff, could you tell me about the people who live in the castle upon the bluff above you?" he questioned.

A cold shadow came over the German's round face. It was evident that at heart he was anything but a genial man given to much talk.

"I do not make my head ache about what I don't know," he replied; "my business is to cook for whoever pays me. That's all I say."

"Oh! I see!" exclaimed Jim, somewhat taken aback. He noticed that Frau Scheff seemed somewhat uneasy, but nevertheless she made no effort to speak.

"Herr Scheff, how about that man with the gray suit, for whom you got a lunch to-day, shortly after noon?" asked John Berwick.

For a moment the German's face took on a decided pallor, and then his expression took on a blank, noncommittal look. There was no getting behind that stolid wall. He shook his head heavily.

"I know nothing about that; maype you are a reporter, eh?"

John Berwick laughed heartily.

"You do me too much honor, Herr Scheff," he said; "I have not the gifts of imagination or the requisite nerve for such a profession."

"Ach! but Fritz—" his wife began, but she stopped with a sigh at the malevolent look her husband shot at her.

Not willing to make trouble for the kind-hearted German woman, Jim and his friend refrained from making any further inquiries. In the course of time they finished their meal, and prepared to leave, feeling like new men and fully ready physically for anything that might be in store for them. The proprietor had regained his surface good humor, and seemed anxious to make the two strangers forget his abruptness.

As for his wife, she was her usual warm-hearted self, and there were tears in her eyes when she said good-by to Jim. "Don't forget my little Fritz," she urged, and Jim promised, and this seemed to give her much comfort.

The two comrades then left the warm shelter of the curious little restaurant. Outside it was misting heavily, but little did they mind it, as they were warm and dry and well-fed. Indeed, they were now doubly anxious to make an end of their strange adventure.

"Herr Scheff was a very uncommunicative old bird," remarked Jim, dryly, as they trudged over the wet, heavy sand towards the cliffs.

"Just what was to be expected," replied John Berwick; "you might just as well try to get water out of the Sahara as information out of Herr Fritz. He would give the devil a meal as quick as he would a parson and ask no questions for conscience' sake. You would never find out that he had ever entertained either. That's business with that class, you know."

"Business be hanged, then!" exclaimed Jim hotly. "I bet anything that the poor man we found murdered in the gulch up here did get a meal from him."

"Certainly," replied the engineer coolly; "and what's more, he knows a whole lot about the gang that infests that castle on the cliff."

"Well, the old clam can keep his information," remarked Jim. "I propose to find out for myself what these rascals are up to. That's the only way."

"You are right there, Jim," replied Berwick.

"We want to go a little careful now," remarked Jim, as they came to the mouth of Dead Man's Gulch.

Noiselessly the two comrades climbed up the dark cleft, over the slippery rocks, until Jim came to a halt.

"That man isn't here now, John," he said in a low voice.

"They've sneaked him off while we were below," remarked the engineer. "It behooves us to be on the lookout."

Somehow, the disappearance of the body of the dead man seemed to give a sense of danger that was everywhere present in the darkness, as if their enemies, though elusive, were near at hand.

"Well, here we are," exclaimed Jim, with a breath of

satisfaction, as they reached the tall fence surrounding the castle on the bluff.

CHAPTER XVIII

THE RECONNOITER

"It seems to me that we are only where we were before," said the chief engineer, in a low voice.

"We won't be there much longer," remarked Jim, with determination; "follow your leader, and look out for the dog; he bites."

This time James Darlington took a new tack, crawling along in the opposite direction from the big gate and keeping well hidden. Followed by John Berwick, he went cautiously along for a distance of a hundred yards, and then Jim halted, and with very good reason, for he had come to the edge of the cliff, but not exactly to the end of the fence.

There was an iron obstruction in the way, that barred them from getting further. It was a fan-like spread of sharp iron spikes, such as you sometimes see in these days, separating the roofs of adjoining tenements on the Island of Manhattan. It appeared an impassable obstacle and indeed it was, as the powerful Jim and the agile engineer had to admit after a careful investigation.

"No use impaling ourselves on that thing," said Berwick. "It's pretty clear that the folks in there don't wish to be disturbed."

"More reason for disturbing 'em," asserted Jim briefly. "That Mexican is inside and has my valued possessions. I intend to get them back."

"I admit the logic, go ahead."

It might have been possible for Jim to have scaled the high fence with its pointed iron spikes, but it was not practicable for the shorter John Berwick.

For a little while Jim sat on the ground thinking, trying to find some way out of the difficulty.

"If we only had a rope," remarked the engineer; "we could make it."

"Yes," replied Jim, "and then use it to hang the greaser with. That is what I call a beautiful thought."

"We haven't enough clothes to spare, to tear up, either," put in Berwick.

"You are right, John," remarked Jim. "It is a little bit too damp and foggy for that."

Jim began pacing up and down for a few minutes, then he reached some decision.

"You stay here, John, for a few minutes," he said.

"I hate to stay alone here in the dark," remarked Berwick humorously.

Jim grinned, then he strode away along the cliff, and quickly disappeared in the darkness. Five, ten, fifteen minutes passed, and then he appeared unexpectedly in front of the engineer.

"Hello, what have you got there?" inquired Berwick; "looks to me like you were going to start a garden."

"I found these vines growing over some rocks back there," Jim explained; "as we haven't any rope they are next best."

"Good boy! I would never have thought of that," said Berwick.

"We have used it before," said Jim; "when we were on the frontier."

"But will it hold?" remarked the engineer. "I'm no heavy weight, but I am not a fairy either."

"Wind 'em together and they will do," replied Jim.

In a short time, he had got one end of the improvised rope over one of the iron spikes, then he criss-crossed them and got the other end over the next spike, making a very respectable ladder.

"You first, John," ordered Jim.

"All right, me lad, and if those hounds in the yard nab me, you must do something to distract their attention."

"I'll attend to them," replied Jim confidently.

"Here goes, then," said the engineer, and with the liveliness of a cat he was up and over, and Jim followed.

"Now," exclaimed the engineer, "we are in for it. What is our next move?"

"Take in this rope," replied Jim practically; "maybe we can use it in our business."

His friend patted James on the back to show his appreciation. Then they together got most of the vine down, and Jim made a neat coil of it. Then before they went on they waited, listening for any sound that might indicate life of any kind about the castle, but it was absolutely dark and silent.

In all probability the dogs were somewhere about, or at least one of them would surely be on guard. Jim knew that the first thing to do was to locate these hounds, for if they were to get on their trail the game would be up, aside from the danger of being attacked by these ferocious beasts, who were in reality as strong as a mountain lion and much more courageous.

First they must find some sort of shelter. The enclosed yard was a large one, including about eight acres, with trees and shrubs set here and there and a fountain in the center of the driveway. This latter they would hardly use, unless they needed a bath. Where the two comrades had got over the fence was on the north side of the house, and about one hundred and fifty yards distant.

At half the distance to the house was a clump of bushes in the center of which rose a tall tree. Back of the castle a short space was a stable built of brick. At first Jim thought of making it his base of retreat and observation but gave it up for the present as he was fearful that one of the dogs might be there or chained near it. As a matter of fact, one of the big hounds was lying with his nose to the ground not far from the double door of the stable. It may as well be stated that this building was at the foot of a sharp slope below the castle and its back wall was built on a line with the bluff.

"Come on, John," said Jim finally; "we will make for that clump of bushes with the tree in the center."

"Aye, aye, sir!" replied the engineer softly.

Jim threw himself on the ground and began to crawl imperceptibly towards the bushes and the engineer followed in as close an imitation of his leader as possible, and about six feet behind him. The grass was four or five inches high and they looked to be only a couple of inconspicuous and inoffensive logs. Jim did not make the mistake of cranching swiftly through the darkness, for motion was the one thing that would attract the attention of even an unwary eye. So much James had learned from his old-time enemies, the crafty and patient Indians.

Once they got a bad scare when they had worked along for half the distance undertaken. Jim and his comrade became aware of the hulking yellow form of one of the huge hounds, as he stalked into the open about fifty yards from where they lay in the short grass. Luckily what little wind there was blew from the southwest, so that it could not aid to betray them.

The beast evidently did not have them in mind, and was unsuspicious of their nearness, as he was looking in the direction of the big gate, but only a short turn about the grounds and he would pick up their trail and then the two comrades might as well resign from their present position and retire over the fence if possible. It would seem as if he were looking for someone to come from the direction of the road. Then to the relief of Jim and the engineer the hound hulked heavily towards the gate.

When he reached it he placed his fore feet high upon a cross bar and gazed through, evidently on the lookout in a friendly, not an inimical way. Then he turned and loping near to the house disappeared in the direction of the stable, and this gave Jim and the engineer their chance to reach the coveted clump of bushes.

"He is surely looking for someone," said the engineer, as they straightened up in their shelter of overhanging leaves.

"Lucky he wasn't hunting for us," remarked Jim. "It would have been all off if he had."

"Or we would be off," put in the engineer frankly.

"Come on, John; let's crawl through this clump and see what is on the other side," ordered Jim.

"Lead on, MacDuff," assented Berwick.

"My name is plain Duff, I'll have ye to know," replied Jim, catching his friend playfully by the throat.

For some reason they both felt a thrill of high spirits go through them and it showed in their speech and actions. If Jim had stopped to consider he would have remembered that high spirits at a time like this always indicated some unusual peril ahead. It had been so on many previous occasions and this peculiar thrill of every fiber was the distillation of the very wine of danger. They had reached the middle of the clump of bushes; Jim leading, when our friend received the shock of his young life, and it startled him through and through.

CHAPTER XIX

THE CASTLE

Jim's hand as he had crawled forward, clutched the foot of a man who was in hiding in this selfsame clump of bushes. James acted instantly, realizing instinctively the danger, the extreme danger of the situation. He leaped forward for the man's throat and to his utter surprise the body lay perfectly limp.

"Great Heavens!" he exclaimed, "this man is dead."

"It's the poor fellow from the gully, below," said the engineer, after an examination; "there's no mistaking him."

"But how did he get here?" questioned Jim, with suppressed excitement and alarm.

"That's simple," replied his friend. "These bandits who live here, brought the body up at the first convenient chance and left it here for the time being, but they may come for it any time so we had better be on the lookout for trouble.

"We don't have to; it is always on the lookout for us," replied Jim briefly and with truth.

"There's someone directly ahead," remarked the engineer, "or I miss my guess."

"Just wait a minute, Chief," said Jim; "I want to size up this castle before making the next move."

"You don't observe any anxiety on my part to go anywhere do you, Captain?" questioned Berwick.

"Quiet as a kitten," replied Jim with a grin, and then without any further remarks, he crawled past the form of the unfortunate man, until he reached the edge of the copse, and gathering a low bush around his shoulders so that he appeared to be a part of the natural scenery himself, he observed the castle closely with the eye of a trained scout.

The fog was rifted by the wind so that he could see with sufficient clearness the outlines and details of the high brick castle. As has been said, they were on the north side, where there was the large stained glass window that lit the grand staircase, and now shone with a faint radiance.

There was also a line of broad mullioned windows, their round, thick glass in circles of lead, gleaming like opals when the full light was within, but now cold and ghostly in the dimness of the fog-laden night. These windows were some twenty feet from the ground, and Jim's keen eyes regarded them with special interest. Further along and somewhat lower were the smaller windows, evidently of the kitchen, and near the ground several more heavily barred.

After a few minutes of observation, Jim returned to his companion, his mind fully made up.

"Well, James, what do you make of it?" queried his friend.

"I'll make more of it a little later," replied Jim; "I'm going to move on the enemy, right away."

"Very well, I'm ready," remarked the engineer. "When you can't go back with safety or stand still it is a good scheme to go forward."

"But I want you to wait here, John," explained Jim; "there's much less chance with two than one. In case I need you I'll yell."

"If you don't happen to be gagged," replied his friend cheerfully.

"Never you fear about that," returned Jim confidently; "there's none of that gang that is going to get me so quick but that there will be something doing on my part first."

"Nothing surer than that," replied the engineer heartily. "Luck to you, Jim," gripping his hand, "and I'll be in reserve here when you want me."

"Good old Chief," said Jim, returning his friend's grip; "now I'm off."

Without any further words Jim crawled to the edge of the thicket, leaving John Berwick in the grewsome company of the dead man, but Berwick took up a position where he could see the tall, shadowy figure of James Darlington as he advanced straight toward the stronghold of this gang of unmerciful pirates.

"That boy has them all beaten when it comes to unqualified nerve," muttered the engineer to himself; "the best fellow in an emergency I ever saw, and that's something."

James would have felt proud to have heard his friend's eulogy, but his mind was fully taken up with the problem he was facing. He must get into that house without delay; to stand long where he was meant sure detection in a short time. If he had only possessed his revolver, he would have felt more comfortable.

"Have to get or borrow a gun from one of those chaps inside there," he mused with shrewd humor.

He was now directly below the long mullioned window, but as he was not a little birdie with wings, he could not fly, and had to climb.

"Here's luck," he said; "this vine is bigger than I thought it could be. Takes California to grow a vine like a tree and that's a fact."

Indeed, the vine that spread its dark green splendor over the whole north side of the great structure and wrapped itself around the giant chimney had a stem that was more like the trunk of a small tree and very tough and fibrous. Jim did not hesitate, but quickly removed his shoes, and with both free hands, noiselessly climbed up towards the window, sustaining his weight partially on the rough jutting bricks until he finally reached in safety the broad sill of the mullioned window.

"So far so good," he murmured, "now to get inside."

Very slowly and cautiously he pushed on the lower part of the center window and it gave easily enough, the gang in foolhardy security never dreaming that an enemy would dare approach their stronghold, much less come into their very castle. Indeed, their confidence was in some measure justified, for their head and chief, old Captain Broome, was very powerful through this section, had strong friends among the officials in the city and was safe from being bothered by the authorities. As for private enemies, he could very well take care of them himself.

So without any trouble at this point Jim slipped through the window and was within the castle of his bitterest enemy. He let himself down from the window, to a settee, and thence to the floor. By the dim light from the windows he saw that he was in a long, rectangular-shaped room, evidently lined with bookcases, and in the dimness at one end loomed the outline of a huge fireplace. For the moment Jim felt a thrill of excitement go through him. There was something in the fact that he was alone and unarmed in the house of his foes, quite enough to give him this sensation.

Suppose that you were standing in the darkness in a cage where some lions were stretched out asleep but liable to awake at any moment, you might be excused if you had a few shivery thrills, and so it was with Jim.

It was evident that this room was not in general use and our adventurer could not have chosen a better place to land as it were.

He stopped only long enough for his eyes to become accustomed to the lack of light and then he made sure that there was nothing in the room that would serve him for a weapon.

"Might take a dictionary and throw some of the hard words at 'em," he remarked with his usual humorous twist of imagination when in a tight place.

Then he cautiously opened a door which led into a long, wide corridor that was decidedly dark, except at the further end, where shone a faint light. Keeping close to the wall, he went softly along until he came to the main staircase, which surprised Jim with the winding sweep of its magnificence and the beautiful stained glass window above it. But there was that in the large hall below that made him draw back.

There was stretched out on an immense rug, the other hound, his nose between his paws and his watchful, red-rimmed eyes upon the great door leading from the hall to the out-of-doors. No wonder that the sight of him made Jim pause and draw back into the darkness of the upper corridor. One suspicion, and the huge beast would take the staircase in three leaps, and neither quickness, strength nor prowess could have saved Jim if once the hound had caught his trail.

"Gosh, I've got to find a weapon somewhere!" Jim mumbled to himself; "this won't do at all."

By this time his eyes had become thoroughly accustomed to the dim light and as he turned back he stopped and his heart beat with something almost akin to fright. Now our friend James Darlington was not superstitious by nature, but if that dim, silvery white figure was not a ghost, what in Sam Hill could it be?

It stood perfectly quiet to one side and about half way down the hall, evidently looking straight at Jim, but making no move to attack him. What was Jim to do? He could not retreat down the staircase to the main door, for that was to fall into the jaws of the hound. Neither could he reach the library in safety.

CHAPTER XX

THE BANQUET HALL

Then Jim looked up at the wall which was paneled in some light wood and there his eyes saw something that gave him the clue. He straightened up and moved quickly towards the ghostly figure.

"How are you, Brian de Bois Guilbert?" he said as he came up. "I should like to borrow your suit of armor if you don't mind."

The audacity of James. It was a gigantic suit of armor, and for the moment Jim thought of trying to get into it, but he gave it up. Perhaps as a last resort he might use it, to strike terror into the superstitious greasers and cutthroats who were making their foul nest in this once beautiful home.

It would be perfectly useless for him to try and put it on in the hall, for it would make clangor enough to arouse the deaf or the dead. So Jim very gently wheedled the image of the late Sir Brian inch by inch towards the library and finally got it inside. Luckily there was only a few feet to go, but it took Jim the better half of an hour. This incident of the armor goes to show how carefully Jim was looking to a possible chance in the future. Our old college chum, Jim, was certainly strong on strategy.

"Now, you stay here, Brian, old Boy," he said, "until I come back; if you don't I'll Ivanhoe your old block for you."

Then Jim slipped out in the passageway once more, and went immediately to the place in the hall from whence he had sighted the armor man. There on the wall were medieval weapons—battle-axes, swords and poniards. These were what had given Jim his clue as to what the ghostly figure really represented.

"I reckon that I will have to appropriate some of this hardware, before I explore any further."

He finally selected a small and exceedingly keen poniard, also a short, heavy sword, and thus equipped he was ready for what might come, which as he well knew was apt to be the unexpected. As he stood motionless in the dark hall, with its dimmed radiance at one end, he was sure that he heard the faint sound of voices, which is not saying that the voices were faint by any means.

As he went cautiously along, the sound of the voices came no nearer, but they did not grow less distinct. This puzzled Jim exceedingly.

"I'd give my hat to be able to locate this serenade," he remarked to himself; "it sounds most peculiar."

James went slowly along, feeling the wall as he went, and all at once his fingers came to a slight break in the smooth wood, and the voices became slightly clearer and Jim was positive that he heard the thrum, thrum of a guitar. He ran his fingers up and down near the minute break, until they touched a small wooden button. He hesitated a moment before pressing it, not knowing what might happen nor what might possibly be on the other side.

"Nothing venture, nothing have," he said, and standing to one side he pressed the button and the door came quietly back.

"Well-oiled piece of machinery that," thought Jim; "I wonder who uses this stage entrance anyhow."

Then there came distinctly and clear the voices of several men singing a Mexican song and Jim saw several steps leading to a lower level under a low-arched passageway. He also heard besides the singing the low voices of men speaking and the occasional moving of a chair. He was soon to solve this particular mystery.

Moving cautiously along he reached the end of the short passageway and there he saw that it opened on a balcony that ran across one end of a high vaulted room, embellished with a beautifully carved ceiling of oak. As the balcony was quite high up and shut in by big panels of wood about four feet in height, he could not see the floor below.

Jim dared not raise his head to see who were in the room, which was evidently intended originally for a banquet hall and not a den of thieves. However, he was not long in doubt as to what to do, for he slipped the poniard from its sheath, and began to cut a hole through the wood in front of him and it did not take him long to have a place large enough to see perfectly what was going on below. He took one long earnest look.

"Gosh," he muttered to himself, "what a chance, what a chance; if I only had my revolver with me, I'd corner that gang in short order." And so he would.

Now this is what he saw, by the light of a mammoth fireplace filled with great logs that sent a weird, but beautiful light glowing and then wavering in shadows across the high arched ceiling. A few feet back from the wide high fireplace with its roaring flame were four men playing cards. They sat around a table, and three in appearance were villainous cutthroats, probably Mexicans by their dark visages, swaggeringly armed with knives and revolvers, with gaudy handkerchiefs knotted at their throats.

The firelight showed the flash of their cruel eyes and teeth at some stroke of fortune in the play, and Jim, who was not unaccustomed to see and deal with dubious citizens, felt that right below him was the hardest bunch that ill fortune had ever brought across his path. He was not forgetting either the Apaches with whom he and his brothers had enjoyed more than one fracas in the great Southwest.

But what the observer regarded with greatest interest was a group of three well back in the shadow, and he needed none to tell him who that short, squat figure was. He held a guitar, and was accompanying his own songs while the other two joined in the refrain. It was his *bete noir*, the Mexican dwarf who had recently robbed him, and out-maneuvered him on two occasions at least.

Strange to say that if you did not see him, and only heard his voice you would be certain that he was a lithe, Spanish cavalier, of the "oh Juanita" type of lover, for his tone was neither guttural nor harsh but smooth and melodious, and to-night for some reason he was inclined to sentimental songs of the serenade kind, but this reason was soon to appear.

"Who gets the Senorita Manuel, the one who came in the carriage this evening, as though to a ball?" queried one of the players at the card table. The words were spoken at an interval between games.

Jim almost stood up in his sudden enlightenment and wrath but he bethought himself in time and with whitened knuckles he drove the poniard held in his hand deep into the wood of the floor. This, in a mild way served to express his feelings. At the question the dwarf swaggered into the full light of the fire.

"I, Manuel de Gorzaga, will have the senorita, my voice will charm her, and my money please her."

Jim could hardly restrain a scornful laugh at the audacity of the dwarf, but he noticed that though the others regarded him askance they did not ridicule him, but seemed to have a certain fear of his malignity, and his cunning craft. Jim saw that he was clean shaven now and that he moved his head back and forth in front of his hump, like an ugly hooded bird, and his shadow was distorted on the high vaulted ceiling into something horrible and of ill omen. To complete the picture, it is necessary to say that he was dressed in gorgeous fashion in a suit of slashed velvet, and a resplendent sash around his waist.

There was a marvelous celerity in his every movement, so that he was like nothing so much as a richly colored spider, that darts from shadow to pounce upon its victim. Jim vowed that he would not leave the castle that night until the Senorita da Cordova, if a prisoner, was freed from the power of this contemptible creature. But he was to find the adventure which he had planned more difficult than was expected and that was saying a good deal.

"How about the senorita's nice little nurse, Senor Manuel da Gorzaga?" questioned one of the card players, with a sneer. "Perchance that person may have something to say to your pretensions."

The dwarf regarded his questioner with a venomous look and then spat emphatically on the floor, but he gave no reply except by an expressive drawing of his fingers across his throat.

"The Duenna's throat is iron," replied the other speaker to this pantomime; "she guards the captain's treasures like the dragon the golden apples."

"I, too, am valuable to that old shark of the seas," replied the Mexican, in most uncomplimentary terms to his master captain, William Broome. "I know his many secrets, and it was I, Manuel, who got the treasure from that long-legged, white-headed gringo" (Jim grinned at this description of himself), "who would make one meal of the brave captain if it were not for me, who am too wise for his thick head."

"Good for you, Humpty Dumpty," said Jim, under his breath, "you won't have to hire anybody to blow your trumpet for you. Sorry I can't stay, old chap, to hear the rest of your interesting and eloquent speech."

CHAPTER XXI

THE APPARITION

Jim now had one purpose in mind when he gracefully withdrew, and closed the door behind him and stood in the upper hall once more and that was to find where in the castle the Senorita da Cordova was. James waited for a minute in the broad hall, not only to get accustomed to the darkness, but to make sure that there was no one coming, or waiting for him.

Our friend had not been taught by harsh experience to no purpose. Nor had he fought the crafty Indian, and failed to learn something of their strategy. So he closed the door as tenderly as a mother, who fears to waken her sleeping babe, and then stood as still as stone waiting, watching, listening. Well it was that he did so. What was that gray bundle across the hall and lying in front of the door opening into the library?

At first glance Jim thought that it might be the hound, but it was not that. It looked more like a shapeless bundle of old clothes. Then under the directness of his gaze the thing stirred, a head was slowly lifted, and like the gradual resurrection from the cerements of death a figure half rose, and a gaze from the gray hood that seemed to burn was fixed upon him.

Next the figure half raised, moved straight and steadily in his direction, noiselessly, but with terrible intentness, direct towards him. Jim did not move. What was the use? It was his purpose to avoid all disturbance or fracas, which would surely wreck his plan now for the rescue of the senorita. He would see what this creature meant and he merely moved his hands lightly, one to grasp, the other to defend a possible thrust at his heart or throat.

To say that he was cool and unmoved would not be true; his heart thumped and he could feel the blood beat in his ears, but he was not trembling or unmanned, though curious chills crept all over his body. This person had advanced now half the way toward him, moving with the same half bent posture, and the left hand gripping the gray cloth at the throat, forming a hood. Then the woman, within three feet of him, raised her face, and looked at him with the wildest eyes ever set in a human visage. They were shot with horror, terror and an insane desperation. By the half light from the end of the hall Jim could not tell whether she were young or old.

Her face seemed to be lighted by her terrible eyes, and from her robe one lean hand crept, half curved as though to claw. It seemed as if at any instant she might scream and clutch him and something must be done forthwith. Jim returned her gaze soberly, but not defiantly, and there was no fear in his eyes. For a moment she paused, a curious questioning showing in her glance.

"I wish to see and speak to a young girl who has been brought to this place," he said quietly. "I am her friend, and would do neither one of you any harm. You see many things and you believe me and know that I speak the truth."

That was a simple speech, but there was more wisdom in it than appears on the surface. It was spoken directly and was phrased to grip with confidence the woman's poor broken mind; and notice also, that there was nothing to unduly excite her by a show of sympathy or to arouse her by denouncing her oppressors, for she was no doubt another victim who had been held for a ransom that had not been forthcoming.

She made no direct reply to Jim, but only threw her head back and laughed noiselessly with wide opened mouth. Then leaving the spot she glided to the staircase and bent down listening intently. As if satisfied she returned in a moment and beckoned Jim to follow her, which he was only too willing to do.

She was a strange guide and might lead him to his destruction, but he was determined to follow her at all hazards for he must find the senorita and that quickly. So he kept only a short distance behind the gray crouching figure.

Going through the main hall they came to a fairly broad staircase, leading to the third floor, thence along a hall dimly lighted to a narrow winding stair, that brought the two of them to a round platform of stone with rooms on three sides. This place was badly lit by a tallow candle, held by a miner's holder, stuck into the wall.

The woman crouched in front of one of the doors, with a wicket in it, whence Jim heard a low voice repeating something over and over, and the sound of it thrilled him for he recognized it as the voice of the Senorita Cordova, praying softly for deliverance. It pierced through Jim's heart, the pity and the pathos of it, and for a moment his eyes were blinded with tears. The next moment he was himself again, as he well needs be. He pushed gently aside the grating covering the aperture in the door itself, so that he was able to see in. It did not require much of a slit for that purpose, and he was able to get a good look at the interior, which was like a cell, with low arched, white-washed ceiling.

It was not a forbidding room either, for at one end was a latticed window with diamond panes, and in the ivy that grew outside it you might imagine the little birds twittering in the summer time. The floor was covered with a heavy rug and a candelabra of a dozen candles gave a pleasant light. The room or cell was heated by coals glowing in an old-fashioned brazier.

Although there were two persons visible, what fastened Jim's eyes was the figure of the Senorita da Cordova. She was kneeling before a *prie dieu* near the casemented window, in evening dress such as she wore when she got into the carriage. She had supposed that she was going to be taken to her father, and instead had been brought to this desperate castle. Her dress of white was ornamented with lace, and there was a bracelet of odd antique design on her rounded arm that made Jim gasp.

He knew where she had got that. It was his present to her, one of the many treasures that he and the other Frontier Boys had found in that mysterious mountain in the interior of Mexico. Why did she wear it? But in regard to that interesting question he had no time to think at this juncture. She looked pale as she knelt there, but hers was a natural pallor and did not mean fear. The graceful figure with a rope of pearls twined in the dark hair was to remain in James Darlington's memory for many a year.

The other figure was that of a tall, gaunt woman, hard featured with reddish brown hair. Jim noted the powerful looking hands and arms and felt sure that she was not an antagonist to be regarded lightly. At that moment the woman rose suddenly from the chair in which she had been seated and Jim saw that she was nearly his equal in height.

"Is that you, you crazy fool?" she questioned in a harsh voice, coming to the wicket and shoving it back. Jim dodged down, hoping that she would unbolt the door but she did nothing of the kind.

"Oh, ho! you're here are you, walked into the cap'en's trap have you, young fellar? I'll tell you one thing, you'll never get out of this house, because nobody wants you enough to pay a ransom. Got that straight, Bub."

Jim had had all kinds of experiences, but this was the first time that a woman's tongue had begun to be sharpened on him and he did not relish it in the least. He felt small and insulted, so mad that he began to see things zig-zag way and was tempted to do something rash, and in fact he did call out.

"Never fear, Senorita, I will get you out of this place."

He saw her clasp her hands and turn towards the door when the sight of her was eclipsed by the bulk of her jailer.

"So it is you, Senor Jim, with the light head."

"It isn't red anyhow," he replied with humorous indignation.

"Ha, ha," she laughed, "you scored that time anyhow."

Jim took this opportunity to throw his weight against the door with all his strength; it sagged, but the bar held.

The woman was furious as she glared out at Jim.

"I could throttle you, you sassy, long legged cub," she yelled, "only I got orders from the cap'n to stay in this here room, and I obeys him."

She made a quick motion with her hand to a place near the jamb of the door.

"Run, Senor, for your life," cried the poor demented woman; "the Devil and his dogs are coming."

Jim saw that he must make his escape instantly or be caught helpless like a rat in a trap to be done to death. He fled with all his speed, and Jim was no slouch of a runner. Down the narrow stairway he sped, and along the hall to the second floor. The question was, could he reach the library where he had climbed in, before the gang in the banquet hall came rushing up the main staircase.

The chances were against his doing this for the pursuers had only half the distance to go and they would be certain to respond to the alarm with much promptness. The Mexican dwarf was notorious for the swiftness of his attack, so that it looked bad for our friend Jim. He must reach that room or what would happen?

CHAPTER XXII

BRIAN DE BOIS GUILBERT

There was just one thing that saved Jim at this juncture. It was an incident which he did not guess at the time and I am not sure that he became aware of it in later life, and yet there are reasons to surmise that he may have heard of it.

As has not been related, the big guardian of the senorita in the cell high up in the tower, had started to give the alarm to the gang in the banquet hall by pressing a button near the door. James Darlington had seen her make the move to ring, and his alarm had been added to by the cry of warning from the crazy woman. He had to run for his life as the reader well knows.

So much Jim was aware of but he did not see what had happened when the red headed woman started to give the alarm. The Senorita da Cordova was not a cowed and spiritless girl and in spite of the terror of her situation, when she saw the intention of her jailer she glided the length of the cell with remarkable swiftness and caught the arm of the woman. The senorita was not a delicate creature either, and in spite of her apparent pallor, she showed a lithe agility in struggling with this giant of a woman, who had the strength of two ordinary men and was probably nearly the equal of the redoubtable Jim himself.

After a struggle lasting some minutes, the girl was thrown with severe violence against the wall of the cell and lay there stunned and bleeding from a cut on the forehead, but her efforts had given Jim time to reach the library which he had to pass and bolt and lock the door to it, before ever the chase began. Meanwhile the unfortunate woman who had been of so much help to Jim had time to flee to a remote corner of the house, where she would be free from pursuit.

James had determined to make his escape the same way he had gotten in, join his comrade, the engineer, who was outside and together plan a new attack. Perhaps they could get the aid of the Federal authorities.

At that moment Jim's eye fell on the hollow figure in armor which he had dubbed Brian de Bois Guilbert, and he determined instantly to carry out the plan that had first occurred to him, which from its very wildness might spell success. At least try it he would; anything was better than leaving the young Spanish girl in the hands of this evil crew, especially as the Mexican dwarf had openly declared his intention of making love to her.

Hastily Jim lit the wax candles on the mantel, that sent their soft gleam through the long, beautiful room, and gave him sufficient light to work by. Now Jim was not only deft, but desperate. How he got into that suit of medieval armor, he could not tell. It would be doubtful if he could have done so in cold blood, but he was spurred on by the terror of the situation. It was just like a man pursued and in danger of immediate capture by his enemies, who comes to a chasm that in ordinary moments he would not think of attempting to cross, but he leaps it because he has to, or fall into the hands of those who pursue him.

As the renegades rushed through the wide hall, with roar of harsh voices, the big hound in the lead, Jim was nearly all saddled and bridled and ready for the fray. It was with a strange feeling of exultation and also of safety that James Darlington found himself thus accoutered and discovered that he could move with comparative ease in the glittering armor on which shone the lights of the candles from above the fireplace.

It was easy to imagine Jim, who was large enough in his own proper person, and now a figure of gigantic size, to be a hero of old Romance; who with three plumed helmets, unheralded and unknown enters the lists to rescue the oppressed and beautiful heroine from the hands of the ruthless destroyer.

Perhaps Jim was a hero, but I will give a considerable sum to the boy or girl who first finds in the many thrilling narratives of "The Frontier Boys," our friend James spoken of or referred to as "our hero." But to leave this realm of fancy and to come back to the practical world of our narrative.

Jim knew that the time allowed him was apt to be very short before he would be compelled to make his debut in his new character, as the man with the iron jaw, mailed fist and steel legs, so he gripped his heavy sword, which none but he could wield (see Walter Scott, who preceded the present writer by some years). I hope you will forgive this jesting, but Jim was a great hand to make fun in the very presence of danger, a trait peculiar to the American character, and so I may be pardoned for following in his footsteps, for I, too, am an American.

Jim advanced toward the door, and he was thoroughly pleased and encouraged to discover that he could move with comparative ease though not noiselessly of course. But what did a little noise inside the room amount to, when there came the roar of the pursuers outside, for they had returned upon Jim's trail, guided by the hound.

The crisis had now come. The huge beast knew that his prey was inside, and he rushed against the door with all of his maddened bulk, and his great bark boomed through the castle, and filled with fury the Mexican bandits who raged on the outside; then came the voice of their leader.

"Back, you fools," he cried; "away from that door."

They were quick to obey, and at that instant there came the sharp report of a pistol; the bullet splintered through the thick casement but it glanced from Jim's steel breastplate, but this attack aroused him to action. With a thrill and tremor of the nerves which he could not repress, he drew back the bolts and with a cry, the impulse of his humorous excitement, "Desdichado to the Rescue!" he flung the door wide open, and stepped with clanging stride through the smoke into the dimly lit hall.

To have seen that great steel-clad figure moving with sudden life would have struck terror to even the stoutest hearts, and shaken the steadiest nerves. But these superstitious Mexicans were driven almost out of their excitable minds by the sudden horror of this seeming apparition. Of one accord they fled, gibbering, towards the stairs, one falling in a faint from fright before he reached them. Even the dwarf who was not afraid of the Powers of Darkness themselves, retreated slowly, sullenly and suspiciously down the hall.

But there was one of all that gang who did not flee, and that was the valiant hound. He sprang full for Jim as the latter stepped from the room into the hall. Jim was not altogether unprepared for this, for he had reckoned that the hound would be the one to make him trouble. If it had not been for the protection of the armor which he wore it would have gone hard with the youth.

But his own strength with the added weight of his suit of mail enabled him to meet the fierce rush of the beast without losing his footing. It also saved his arm and shoulder from being torn by the grip of the animal's jaws. It only dented him as the expression goes. Then with a short arm thrust of his sword he put the hound out of business. Determined to follow up his advantage and make the rout thorough, he advanced to the head of the staircase.

The dwarf had just reached the foot of the stairs, and looking up he saw the giant figure in armor and with a snarl he took quick aim and fired, the bullet glancing from the helm of Jim's armor and making a long furrow in the plaster of the ceiling.

Jim had no idea of quietly standing there as a tin target for his enemy to fire at. There was, he noted, a small marble bust on a pedestal near the top of the staircase. This he seized in his iron grasp and hurled it at the elfish figure in the hall below. Now James was "quite some" thrower as they say in the state of Jersey. The dwarf was marvelously quick, too, but the white flash of stone came near getting him and as he dodged he slipped and fell and the bust busted in all directions, one fragment cutting his cheek, with its sharp impact.

"Look out, Jim! Look out quick!" so a friend would have cried but it was too late.

While the men had all fled in utter fear, a woman was coming quickly to retrieve their reverse. "Red Annie," as she was known, strong, strident and feared by everyone within the castle, was on the trail. She was not to be fooled for an instant by this figure in armor. Noiseless as a lioness she crept up behind Jim and as he half turned to find another weapon to his hand he saw her, but not soon enough. With a mighty shove she sent him toppling down the stairs. However, Jim was able to partially save himself by gripping at the balustrade.

CHAPTER XXIII

THE CRISIS

There was but one way of escape now and that was by the front entrance. Jim regained his feet but by the time he reached the lower hall, the woman had rallied the brown and white renegades with taunts and fierce ridicule, and they came again into the attack.

"Take him alive," cried the dwarf; "we will have some sport with him before he dies."

"I won't die till my time comes," mumbled Jim; "as for the sport, I'll have that myself."

There were at least twelve of the cutthroats who swarmed into the hall, some of them reenforcements, men who had been sleeping in other parts of the castle, and who had been aroused by the racket. Among them was a huge fellow with a bristling red mustache, close cropped black hair, and sinister dark eyes, all surface and no depth.

"Jack, darlint," cried the woman, "hit that jinted piece of hardware a blow with a shillayleh, and show these Manuels and proud Castilians that it's a holler sham."

"I'll do it for the honor of the ould sod, Annie, me gurl," he cried to his wife, for such she was.

Jim was pretty thoroughly aroused by these taunts, and he did not wait for the onslaught of the gallant son of Hibernia, but plowed his way through the snarling Mexicans, who would have pulled him down, and with a quickness that took the big Irishman by surprise, smote him with a heavy swing upon the side of his fortunately thick head; that is, fortunate for him, and down he went full length, crushing two small, protesting "Manuels" in his fall. He was the victim of the iron hand, minus the velvet glove.

But now a trick was brought into play which Jim himself had used once or twice in the course of his adventurous career. While he was busily engaged with the matter in hand, he suddenly found his arms pinioned by a rawhide lasso, cast by the expert hand of Master Dwarf. In a minute he was utterly helpless, unable to move arms or legs, and then how the Mexicans came into the attack!

With Southern fury they struck at the iron Jim with feet and fist, and then they wrung their injured hands and nursed their bruised toes, until Jim could not help laughing, in spite of the seriousness of the situation; but he did not laugh long.

The ordeal began quickly for him, and he realized that there was no escape for him from the hands of his ruthless and revengeful enemies. It was impossible for John Berwick to help him; indeed, the engineer would be fortunate to escape himself. Besides him, there was absolutely no one within several thousand miles who could bring him help.

If only Jo and Tom and Juarez were near, the old frontier combination, he would not despair of being rescued; but Jim repressed quickly any thought of his brothers and friend, for the recollection would be sure to weaken him, and he needed all his fortitude at this point, when cruel Death and he stood face to face once more, and seemingly for the last time.

It was a dramatic scene, as well as one of terror, in the splendid banquet hall, where Jim awaited execution. The blaze was leaping upward in the great fireplace, and the ruddy spread of light showed the tall figure of James Darlington, bound hand and foot, with his back to the northern end of the banquet room. The armor had been torn off from him with bruising force. The side of his face was torn and bleeding, the work of Red Annie's husband when his opponent was helpless.

Jim had steeled himself for what must come, and he had to admit that he would just as soon be back in Colorado in the hands of the Indians as in the power of the present gang. At least as far as the dwarf was concerned, there was more of personal hatred than in the case of the red men. And where natural cruelty is urged on by a desire for revenge, then look out.

"We will try this game first," cried the dwarf, "and see how brave this white-headed gringo is."

The others laughed and made wagers on their skill, all except the Irishman, who glowered at the Mexicans and then at Jim. It was not a pastime he was expert in. The hunchback took a step forward with his dagger poised over his shoulder, and holding it by its sharp tip. Then it flashed red straight for Jim's eye, apparently, but it would have missed his head by a hair's breadth if he had stayed quiet.

But he was free to move his head and instinctively he dodged; this roused the Mexican to perfect fury, and he grabbed a poniard from the man next to him, and aimed for the body. There was murder in his every move, there was no mistaking that. It looked as if Jim's time had certainly come.

But what of John Berwick, the former chief engineer of the *Sea Eagle*? Why did he not make some effort to aid his friend, and superior officer, Captain Jim? Let us go back a ways, and we will find an answer to this query. As you remember, when Jim started to find his way into the castle, he left Berwick in a clump of bushes not far from the house.

In one way he was alone, and in another he was not, for there was the body of the unfortunate secret service man, who had lost his life in the gulch below, not far from the beach. But most people would have chosen to be alone rather than in such company.

The engineer watched Jim as he climbed up to the broad window and disappeared with a wave of his hand. For a time he listened, on edge for some outbreak, and expecting every minute to see Jim take a flying leap from some window, accompanied by a salute of fireworks and pistol flashes. Once or twice he was positive that he heard a cry or a sound of a struggle in the great silent house, but nothing came of it.

It was cold standing there, motionless. He did not want to attract possible attention by moving about, and a thought came to him upon which he acted. His silent companion had no use for apparel. He secured the heavy gray coat and put it on over his own. His hat he had lost, and substituted that of the officer.

An hour or more went by. He found himself growing very sleepy, and no wonder, if we recall what a strenuous twelve hours he had just gone through. Nor did he have the stimulus of interest that Jim had to keep him keyed up. He fought against this sense of overpowering drowsiness, that was like a heavy adversary that was slowly pressing him into unconsciousness.

It had him by the wrists tiring him, weighing on the pit of his stomach, numbing the back of his brain, making his limbs as heavy as ponderous lead. It seemed to the wearied engineer that there was nothing in this world to be desired but a good sound sleep; he fought against it desperately, but after a long struggle he suddenly succumbed; his head dropped, and he lay prone in the grass, apparently as lifeless, as the unfortunate a few feet distant.

When he awoke it was with utter bewilderment. Where was he, with grass and trees and shrubs all about him? That certainly was a pistol shot which had aroused him. Then he came to his senses, sprang quickly to his feet, and pushed his way through the copse until he got a clear view of the castle. There he saw faint gleams of light through the broad windows of the room, which Jim had entered.

In a moment he had heard enough to convince him that there was serious business going on in the castle, and that "the captain," as he sometimes called Jim, was in certain danger. Now, John Berwick did not have the natural headlong courage of Jim, but he was a man of great coolness and nerve, when the occasion demanded it. He resisted the impulse to rush boldly into the house, for he saw that it would be foolhardy, as he was unarmed, and it would only be making a bad matter worse.

He stood with his head slightly bent, gently whistling to himself; his hands in his pockets, as if nothing of importance was going on in the gloomy, looming castle a few feet away, but John Berwick was thinking, and his thinking, it chanced, was apt to be to some purpose. Then a curious smile came over his face, that was not exactly pleasant, and with fair reason.

The engineer had come to a decision, and hit upon a plan. He and the dead man were about of the same build, practically of the same height, and superficially they had a similarity of appearance, and he was dressed in his coat and hat. The latter he grasped firmly and pulled well down over his face. The coat and hat were the only conspicuous things about him.

Just now there was a sudden terrible clangor in the castle.

"Sounds like somebody was discharging the cook," he remarked with whimsical humor, "and that she was throwing the hardware around."

This tumult, as the reader well knows, was our esteemed friend, James, falling downstairs in his full suit of armor, which was sufficient to account for the racket. It did not take Berwick long after that to get ready, and you would have been certain that it was none other than the dead detective come to life, as he stooped hurriedly across the lawn. He did not try any roundabout way of making entrance into the castle, but ran directly to the massive front doors, hoping to find them unlocked, but in this he was doomed to disappointment.

CHAPTER XXIV

A REINCARNATION

It was no time to waste any precious moments on ceremony; he must act, and act immediately. There were on either side of the main door long panels of glass. John Berwick made use of the stout stick, his only weapon, which he had picked up from the midst of the copse, and broke the long panel glass into smithereens.

Under ordinary conditions the noise would have been sufficient to attract the attention of anyone in the banquet hall, in spite of the heavy doors and their equally heavy hangings of cloth of purple, but at this precise moment the parties therein were so intent on the tragedy that was about to be consummated there, that they would not have been diverted by even a much louder noise than that caused by the breaking of that slender panel of glass.

John Berwick was of slight and wiry figure, and was able to shove his way through, a feat that would have been impossible for Jim, even with the most determined intentions in the world. Within a half minute Berwick stood crouching in the hall, and then he crossed the space swiftly, through the open door, the purple curtains parted, and there advanced into the center of the banquet hall, the gray-clad figure seemingly of the dead detective.

The deadly dagger which the Mexican Dwarf poised to transfix his victim was never flung, but dropped with a metallic clatter from his palsied hand. Even Jim was dazed for a few seconds by this strange apparition, and then he could have given a yell of joy and of boundless relief. It was one of the few dramatic moments of his life, which had been filled with exciting incidents, which is an entirely different thing from being dramatic.

The first look at John Berwick, wearing the detective's coat and hat, the latter pulled well over his face, had appalled and paralyzed the gang of dastards, who were about to execute cold-blooded murder, and as he advanced upon them this fear was changed into frenzied panic. Trampling over one another at once they fled by way of a door at the end of the room, near where they were gathered. The supposed detective gave up the pursuit after they were utterly routed, and returned to where Jim stood bound.

"How did you ever think of it, old chap?" cried Jim, as soon as the rope that bound him had been cut by his friend.

"It chanced that I was prepared," replied Berwick. "I heard that horrible clatter in the house, and got in as quickly as I could."

"That clatter was Brian de Bois Guilbert tumbling down-stairs," said Jim gleefully.

"Eh?" questioned Berwick, his eyes opening wide as he gazed at Jim in the dawning belief that the experience he had gone through had unsettled his mind.

"Oh, I'm not crazy, Chief," exclaimed Jim. "I'll explain later;

now for getting the senorita out of the hands of these villains."

"She is here? Then I'm ready," rejoined Berwick, "but let's get a weapon or two before we start. We may need them."

Jim had now regained the use of his stiffened muscles, and together the two comrades went to the end of the long room.

"This is yours, Jim," he said, as he stooped and picked up the weapon which the Mexican had dropped.

"Sure it is," replied James. "My friend, Manuel, was about to hand it to me."

"It's poisoned, look out for it," said the engineer, as he handed the blade to him gingerly.

"Here's a revolver," cried Jim, "that one of the gents dropped in his hurry. Shy only one cartridge, too," he concluded, after a hasty examination.

Thus equipped, they started on their quest, and though very inadequately armed they both felt heartened by the presence of the other. It is a desolate business, facing danger alone with no one to back you up, or with whom you can take counsel. True comradeship is one of the best things in the world.

The two friends move quickly across the floor, but, by comparison with the danger that is approaching, they seem merely to crawl. You long to shout a warning to them, do anything to urge them on. They reach the door of the banquet hall, and then they are quick to act, and with good reason.

"What durned son of thunder broke that thar glass?" There

was no doubt whose voice that was. It belonged to the redoubtable Captain Broome, and to no other. It was his stopping to look at the broken glass that gave the two comrades their chance.

"Busted in'ard," he commented shrewdly, and then his gray, red-rimmed eye, with its gleam of steel, caught sight of Jim and the engineer, as they came through the door of the banquet hall. With a roar of wrath he was inside, followed by six of his sailors; then his humor changed as he saw Jim looking down from the head of the stairs.

"Very good of you, Mr. Darlington, to visit me in my humble home; sorry I wasn't here to welcome you," he remarked suavely.

"Oh, I've made myself quite at home, Captain," replied Jim. "Nice place here; wouldn't you like to trade it for my fine sea-going yacht in the harbor?"

The captain grew red in the face at this piece of persiflage, and under the stress of excitement he swallowed his quid of tobacco and likewise his wrath, at Jim's coolness.

"Waal, son, that's extra kind of you, ain't it, boys?" and he looked over the hard beaten crew at his back.

A loud guffaw of derision greeted this remark, and it was Jim's turn to feel like swallowing something, only it was not a quid of tobacco, for that was a foreign substance he never indulged in, but he made another bold move by way of reply.

"Well, Captain, as you won't consider a dicker with me, I've got a friend with me who represents the United States government. Perhaps he will buy your chalet here by the sea."

John Berwick, who had been standing in the shadow back of Jim, gave a grunt of surprise at the audacity of this move, but he was game, and stepped quietly into the limelight. Captain Broome stood for a moment in open-jawed surprise, and then he dropped his byplay of grim politeness with startling suddenness. A shot rang out, and a puff of smoke drifted across the hall. The bullet zipped close to John Berwick's head.

"Don't fire yet," warned Jim; "come quick."

He led the way swiftly down the hall, determined to make one last effort to save the senorita, though it would have been easy enough for him to have saved himself and his comrade by dashing into the library, barring the door, and climbing down by the way which he had come up, but to Jim's credit, be it said, the thought of such escape never crossed his mind.

As they ran, Jim had the presence of mind to swerve for a second and grab the hound which he had killed a short time before and drag it out so that it lay crossways of the hall; then on they dashed, while the lumbering sailors, better for climbing masts than for sprinting, came awkwardly on their trail.

The pursuers had only started on the level of the hall when a volley of six shots flashed in sudden flame in the direction in which Jim and his friend were running. Two came unpleasantly near, but this only added a zest to the race, and Jim laughed with a snort of disdain.

"You fellows shoot like Chinamen," he yelled in derision, which remark reached the ears of Captain Broome and his gang with forcible distinctness. It served to blind them with fury, and the next moment the captain fell forward over the dead hound, and three of his gallant sailors sprawled over him, for which piece of awkwardness they were berated and kicked and cuffed by their irate employer.

"What dumb fool left that hound there!" he yelled when he saw the obstruction by the light of a full lantern that one of his men lit. "He's been pizened."

"Cut in the neck, Cap'n, that's what killed the beastie."

It was only too true, as the old pirate saw, and he went into a fit of rage that left him inarticulate; but from the way he shook both gnarled fists in the direction in which Jim had fled, it was clear that he knew who was responsible for the death of his hound, and who had placed it where it was. With a sudden sense of superstition his memory went back to the fate of his great gorilla of the cavern that once had guarded his treasure in a cave in one of the islands off the coast of California. It was this same big, humorous, blond-headed boy, who had several times outwitted and beaten him, though not always, for the hard-bitten old salt horse had now gotten his yacht back from Jim's grip, and, through one of his agents, had a few days ago relieved him of his treasure. Now, in spite of daring and long-headedness, the captain seemed likely to defeat the youth's present intention of freeing the Senorita da Cordova from his cold, calculating and cruel grip.

At least it was not certain that James Darlington was to win her release; however, he had before fought against odds quite as desperate and won. We shall see. However, there was no question as to the bitter chagrin of Captain Bill Broome as he took up the broken pursuit.

CHAPTER XXV

IN THE CELL

James did not stop to gloat over the momentary holdup of his enemy, but followed by his comrade, he sped around the turn of the hall, then up to the second story to the narrow winding stairway, winding between stone walls, towards the cell where the senorita was under guard of the tall, red-headed Amazon.

As he reached the landing a bitter surprise awaited him. The door of the room was wide open. Not a soul was there. The bird had flown. Instantly Jim turned and started to descend the stone stairs. What his intentions were it would be difficult to say. It would have been a long and hard task to have found out in which room, out of the many, the senorita was now held prisoner, even if he had had leisure to look, but under the circumstances with enemies on all sides it was impossible.

Already the captain and his men were near the foot of the winding stair, and from the other direction came some of the panic-stricken Mexicans, who had heard the voice of Captain Broome ringing through the house.

It doubtless gave them renewed courage to find that he was

on deck; besides, they would have been afraid to have him discover them lurking in fear about the premises, and then, too, they had motives of their own for joining in the chase now that reenforcements had arrived.

"Back up, Jim," cried John Berwick; "the dogs have got us cornered."

"Hold 'em off," exclaimed Jim; "take one shot; save the rest."

He leaped back to see what way of escape there might be without retreating into the *cul de sac* of the cell. He caught a projection in the stone above the landing in an effort to reach the glass skylight. At that moment there came a quick shot below him, and the report roared and reechoed in the winding stairway. There was a yelp like that of a wounded animal, and one of the Mexicans fell backward down the stairs, not mortally wounded, as he thought he was.

For a moment the mob was held back, and then Captain Broome himself took the lead; he contributed the force and fury of the charge, and the Mexicans the loud yells and exclamations of burning wrath.

"This is the only way out, Jim," cried Berwick, making for the empty cell. "No time to waste climbing up stone walls."

Jim saw the force of this; he leaped down to the landing, and as the leaders of the charge came surging around the curve in the stone stairway, he and Berwick rushed into the cell, slammed and barred the door, as the enemy came against it with a dull thud.

There was no chance to make a barricade, as there was scarcely any furniture in the cell. Nothing would have pleased Jim better than that means of defense. There were just two things to do, either surrender or to try the window.

Jim would never think of the first; death was better than that. It was only a question of a few minutes before the door would be down and their capture or death certain. Nothing needed to be said. Jim put out the dim lamp as Berwick reached the leaded casement window.

In a moment they were out on a narrow balcony of iron, but green with ivy and a rambler rose, that hung and nodded near the casement. The dim light of morning was seeping through the heavy folds of fog, and spreading in steel-like patches over the dark-hued Pacific.

Even in this moment of danger they were glad to breathe in the fresh air. If only the fog was thicker it might be of help to them; if they had only looked landward their hearts would have been lighter, for there in huge rolls of gray the fog was moving, thick, impenetrable, over the ground, and in a short time, probably not over a minute, the castle and the whole coast would be enveloped.

But the two had to do something immediately, and could not stand there admiring the scenery. Above them rose the high peak over the window, and higher yet the hip of the roof. A glance was sufficient to show Jim that they did not want to get up any higher in the world than they were. Below them was the ridge of another roof, about a distance of a dozen feet; a dizzy drop, but they had to do it; there was no other way.

"I'll go first," determined Jim, "and then you follow."

At that instant, a red glow shone through the thick round glass of the casement, and the door fell with a crash. Jim climbed out, and holding to the lower edge of the balcony, without the slightest hesitation, dropped. His feet struck on the slant, and his hands gripped the ridge and he pulled himself up. The engineer was already dangling in the air, holding on to the edge.

"Now," cried Jim.

A moment after the casement had burst out, the engineer let go, Jim steadied him as he struck, and exerting all his strength barely kept the two of them from sliding down and out. The fog was already upon them with its thick enveloping whiteness, and they could not see more than two feet in either direction. It was indeed a case where fortune appeared to favor the brave.

"They're down there all right," cried the captain in his harsh voice; "we've got 'em where they can't get away. Don't shoot, lads, we'll take 'em alive."

A roar of approval met this declaration.

"Give me a lasso, Manuel, and hurry, or I'll take the end of it to you," roared the captain.

Jim put his hand on his comrade's shoulder and whispered:

"I want that lasso," and he edged along until he was directly underneath the balcony, then he rose slowly to his feet, which, in his wet stockings, did not slip. Manuel, indeed, had hurried, for no sooner had Jim risen to the height of his precarious position than he saw the rope dangling downward like a snake. He let it alone until he believed that it was paid out to the full.

Then he gripped it with both of his powerful hands, and gave it a yank, as though he were ringing out the old year. It pulled the sailor who was paying the rope out bodily out of the balcony, and only the agility and strength of the captain kept him from falling into the hands or upon the head of the enemy below, but in the struggle he let go of the rope.

Jim, with his treasure firmly in hand, now moved rapidly along the ridge of the roof to a chimney, paying no attention to the uproar on the balcony above, nor to the shots that, with a dimmed report, tore harmlessly through the gray garment of the fog. It did not take them long to tie the rope around the chimney and then Berwick slid down past several windows and with a drop of ten feet was on the ground once more. In a moment Jim was standing by him. His first act was to seek out and put on his shoes.

"Over the fence now, Captain?"

"No," replied Jim, "we won't give up the fight till we're beaten."

"Better get, while we have the chance," protested the engineer earnestly.

"Come quick; I have a scheme," announced Jim. "We won't run yet."

"No faster than molasses in January," said the engineer irritably.

"Take it easy, John," said Jim soothingly, with a pat on the shoulder; "we'll come out all right, my boy."

It was as though Jim were the older of the two, but it was the quality of leadership in him that made him hearten his comrade. Berwick responded, his good nature instantly restored.

"Go it, Cap. I'll see you through this if it takes my head and both feet."

"Thank you, John," replied Jim, gripping the other's hand. "It won't be as bad as that, I hope."

Then they started directly for the fence, to the complete surprise of the engineer, for Jim had declared against that route most emphatically; but Berwick made no protest, for, as James had said that he had a scheme, he knew it would soon develop. He noticed that his leader made no effort to disguise his footprints as they ran, and so it was not a shock to him, when they reached the fence, to see that Jim made no attempt to scale it. He stopped a moment to listen for any sign of pursuit.

CHAPTER XXVI

IN THE MOW

"All quiet along the Potomac," remarked Jim, as no disturbance was heard from the direction of the house.

"Not a sound was heard, not a funeral note," added the engineer, with his usual whimsical humor.

"I bet that there will be a few funeral notes for that fellow who let go the rope," put in Jim.

"Not to speak of what would happen to us if old Broome should get his hand on we 'uns," remarked the engineer casually.

"He's just mad enough to chaw iron," grinned Jim. "Well, now, here's for a little acrobatics."

Jim leaped up to the stone and cement parapet in which the iron fence was set, taking care to leave a few mud traces on the cement; then he went along for some little distance from iron bar to iron bar, and when he rested he did not do so on the wall, so that all trace of their trail was practically lost, even to the nose of a bloodhound. John Berwick followed him with greater agility than Jim showed, for he was much lighter, and very wiry, so that it was easy work for him compared with the heavier Jim.

Berwick did not guess what their destination might be, though he had some idea that Jim's scheme was to get down to the beach, but how this was to be done without getting outside of the grounds he could not figure. Then close by he saw the faint outline of a building through the fog, and he thought for the moment that they had come back to the house; however, he recognized it as the stable. This building was a rustic affair, built with logs that still had the bark on, and had originally cost much more than a stone or brick structure would.

"Here we are," said Jim in a low voice; "now look out for the hound."

"I don't believe that he is here now," said Berwick.

This proved to be the case, and they were able to slip into the stable without anyone being the wiser. It seemed like a refuge to the two comrades after the hazards that they had run during the past few hours. And even Jim was fagged and worn, and now that there was time for reaction his face showed it. There were deep cuts of fatigue in his cheeks and his eyes looked haggard. They also burned, and his head was full of a sort of vacant daze, from sleeplessness.

"I don't know, John, whether I'm hungrier or sleepier, but if I had to choose I think that I would select a nap."

"You have had it a lot harder than I have, old chap," said the engineer; "take a lay-off and get some sleep."

"I believe I will," agreed Jim; "I don't imagine that we will be disturbed for some time at least."

There was plenty of hay in the warm, dusky mow, and a cozy, safe place to rest in.

"I tell you what, Chief," said Jim, "let's both take a sleep, and then we will be fresh for what may happen next."

"It wouldn't take much urging," replied the engineer; "I'm half dead for sleep myself, but we had better make the doors secure first, in case they should look for us here."

"No," rejoined Jim, "leave everything open; if they came to the stable and found it locked on the inside, they would know, for sure, that we were in here."

"But suppose some of the gang come in here while we are asleep, they would be certain sure to hear one or both of us snoring."

"That's right enough," agreed Jim, "but I tell you what we can do, we'll crawl down under the hay, get close to the wall, and our loudest snores would be smothered."

"I guess you're right," agreed Berwick. "So lead on and I will follow."

"This reminds me of when I was a boy," declared Jim; "when we used to tunnel in the hay to hide in the old barn on the back lot."

"When you were a boy," exclaimed Berwick, in good-natured raillery. "How old do you consider yourself now, I should like to know?"

"Oh, I've lived in heartbeats, not in years," said Jim; "that makes me about a hundred years old."

"It strikes me that it takes a good deal to make your heart beat faster than usual," remarked the engineer; "you are a cool hand if there ever was one." This was a sincere tribute.

Then the two comrades began to work back under and through the hay, keeping close to the south wall, so that the hay showed no sign of having been disturbed, and in a short time they had burrowed their way clear through, until they reached the back wall. How comfortable and cozy it was in the warm, dry hay! Jim stretched his weary length out with a sigh of relief.

"Ah, John, isn't this great? After being through what we have," exclaimed Jim.

"It is fine," agreed Berwick, "to get into a safe, warm place like this when you have been in constant danger, as we have, and cold and wet besides. Here goes for a good sleep."

And the word was hardly out of his lips when he was sound asleep. Jim looked at his watch by means of a crack of light that came in between the logs, and saw that it was twenty minutes after six. And then, lulled by the sound of the waves at the base of the cliffs, he too sank into a deep, dreamless sleep.

He never thought of sleeping beyond a couple of hours, but he had not counted on the effect of his extreme fatigue, and the sudden cessation of the constant strain the two had been under for nearly eighteen hours. So hour after hour went by and still they slept in the cozy and soft dryness of the hay, that has no equal as a bed for the truly weary.

It was after two in the afternoon that something happened that roused them; otherwise they might have slept until night, and indeed it was almost as dusk as night, for the fog which had lifted in the morning closed in thicker than ever, so that in the homes and offices of the city the gas lamps and jets were burning.

Jim awoke with a start, utterly and absolutely bewildered. Where he was he could not guess; his mind was a confused daze of fragments of events that had happened during the night of adventure and excitement. Then he came to himself and remembered how they came in this strange place. His hand reached out and touched the foot of his sleeping comrade. But what had roused him? There had been something; of that he was certain. So he kept perfectly still, listening with the utmost intentness; then he started slightly, for there was repeated the noise that had roused him from his sleep. It was a low, terrible croon, like "o-o-h—o-o-h," repeated and repeated, and every once in a while its monotone was broken by a sharp shriek.

Rested though he was, and not liable to nervous tremors, Jim felt his flesh creep at the uncanny sound. It came, as far as he could judge, from the open space in the mow not far from the ladder that led up into the loft. But what it was he could not guess, nor its object in coming to this particular spot. One thing was probable, that it had nothing to do with them, and was not indicative of someone on their trail, but it was no pleasant companion to have in that dusky loft.

He wished that John Berwick might wake, but he did not want to disturb his much-needed rest until necessary. At that moment there came that horrid shriek, and, as if in reply to it, the engineer struggled up with a loud yell. Jim had to shake him vigorously to bring him out of his very natural nightmare. The sound outside had suddenly stopped, and Jim heard a rustling, creeping noise, and then all was silence.

"What in the deuce was that?" whispered Berwick.

Jim made no reply, only put his hand on his friend's shoulder. He could imagine this object rising up and peering through the dusk, trying to make out what that other noise might be, then evidently not much worried about it. After a short interval, it began its peculiar croon again.

"I don't know what it is, John," replied Jim to his friend's repeated question; "it has been going on some time before you waked. You must have heard it in your sleep, and that is what gave you that nightmare."

"It must have been that," remarked the engineer, "because it could not have been anything that I have eaten." There was no doubt about the humor of this. They were able to talk together in low tones, for this object outside seemed to be more concerned with its own troubles than anything else.

"How long have we slept?" queried Berwick.

"Bless me if I know," replied Jim, "and it is so dark in here now that I can't make out the time."

"Well, I reckon that it is high time to get up, anyhow," remarked Berwick.

"It is more a question of getting out than of getting up," remarked James, with his usual quaint humor.

But at this point Berwick put a hand of caution on Jim's shoulder, for he was sure that there was something on hand.

CHAPTER XXVII

LOOK DOWN AND NOT UP

THE engineer was entirely right. There was somebody knocking at the gate, as they are wont to say in romantic novels, but in this particular case it was the barn doors where the noise was heard. They were rolled back and then came the sound of loud voices, or, to be accurate, they were rather shrill.

"That's the Mexicans," declared Berwick; "they are on our trail."

"We will make them get off," remarked Jim grimly.

"Better throw them off," said the engineer wisely.

"Gosh ding, I don't see how we are going to get out of here now if they decide to make a search of the premises," remarked Jim; "we are in for it."

John Berwick was on the point of saying something about "I told you so," but he thought better of it, for you remember that it had been his idea to fasten the stable when they first came in. "I guess the only thing for us to do is to make a rush for it when they discover us," said Jim, "and trust to our luck which seems uncommon bad of late."

"Due to turn," said Berwick; "it's run against us long enough."

The men's voices below had suddenly ceased, and then there were signs of a vigorous search on the lower floor. It was only a question of a little time when the search would reach the hay loft, where our two friends were in hiding, and then—

"I'm going to crawl around and see if I can't find some way of getting out of this trap," declared Jim.

"All right, I'll stay here and guard our common fireside," replied the engineer with his queer twist of humor.

"Speaking of firesides," remarked Jim; "if they would only set fire to this place they would surely get us."

"It would be a case of roast pig, as Charles Lamb says," put in John Berwick.

"The two would go well together, was he a sheep or a mutton," said Jim coarsely, for be it known James was not much of an authority on English literature, the only classics with which he was fully acquainted being, "The Frontier Boys in Every Part of the World," which, with Shakespeare, forms a complete library.

"I fear you are nothing but a Bravo, James," remarked his friend.

"What's that?" Jim inquired. "Some other time will do just as well," he declared, "I am going scouting."

Suiting the action to the word, he started to crawl along the wall, and it did not take him long to get free of the hay, and raising his head, he saw something that made him draw down hurriedly, and take the trail back to where his comrade was waiting.

"What luck?" asked Berwick.

"Not a place where a rat could crawl out," remarked Jim, "but you just wait. I think there is something going to happen."

There did, but it was not exactly what was expected. It was evident that the search below was over, and after a brief parley, heavy feet could be heard coming up the ladder. At the moment that the leader's head appeared through the opening, a gray and ghostly figure rose with its weird, shrill cry of rage that startled the two comrades safely hidden in the hay.

The effect upon the intruders can be easily guessed. These superstitious Mexicans had known vaguely of a woman haunting this castle by the sea. Sometimes they had seen a gray, creeping figure at the end of the hall or heard a piercing cry ring out at midnight, and now this creature was about to spring upon them and curse them to the bottomless pit. There was a cry of fright, and in leaping back, the man near the top of the ladder knocked over the one below, and he in turn the next, so that it was like when a ball hits the King Pin and the others are sent sprawling.

The searching party fled in panic and dismay out of the barn, and nothing could have persuaded them to have set foot in those haunted walls again, no, not even the threats of the redoubtable Captain William Broome himself. What the outcome would have been had the captain been on hand, it is difficult to say, for it was commonly supposed that he was in fear of nothing.

"Well, what did I tell you, Jack?" questioned Jim smiling grimly. "There was something on hand sure enough."

"What under the canopy was that thing doing?" exclaimed John Berwick. "It gave me the creeps, and that is a sensation that does not bother me very much these days."

"That was the story of a haunted house," replied Jim, "but it is safe enough now since our friends, the enemy, have fled. Let us go out and see for ourselves if you aren't too timid."

"Anybody who survives the excitement of following your fortunes for a few weeks cannot be very timid," replied Berwick candidly.

Jim grinned, but made no reply, and in a few moments they emerged from the hay into the dusk of the loft. For a few seconds they made out nothing, and then from the deeper shadow a dim figure took shape, and advanced towards them. Jim was the nearest to her, and Berwick was very well pleased that this was so. Jim showed no uneasiness.

"Thank you for driving them away," he said quietly, peering down at the strange face that looked up at him from its hooded gray, and then she laughed at him with insane mirth. It would have done severe damage to less hardy nerves than those which our "hero" possessed. Jim regarded her with unwavering kindness, which seemed to reach through the gray cloud of her unhappy condition, much as the clear sun penetrates the mist.

"The old devil has gone," she volunteered.

"Ah, the captain," said Jim to Berwick quietly.

"She could mean no other," agreed his friend. "Perhaps we had better follow his example."

"And the young lady?" questioned Jim.

There was a nod of the head, and even while they were speaking, the woman had faded back into the shadows. They did not disturb her, for it would be to no purpose.

"How had we better get out of here, that is the question," continued Berwick.

"I thought we might go out the back way," remarked Jim.

"How, jump?" inquired Berwick, who remembered the cliff, one hundred feet sheer descent, that bounded the precincts of the castle, except that shut in by the iron fence.

"It won't be hard," said Jim, "if we can find a rope around here, and I think we can."

"If we do, we will keep enough to hang the captain with," said Berwick grimly.

"There's a souvenir hanging from the chimney," said Jim with a grin.

"Better leave that for Santa Claus," remarked the engineer thoughtfully.

"Santa Claus doesn't come to California," replied James; "they don't have Christmas weather here."

"Get lost in the fog, that's a fact," remarked Berwick.

"Come," cried Jim, "let us find some rope."

Down the stairs they went, and it did not take them long to discover a tar-hued rope coiled in one of the empty feed bins.

"Here's our treasure," said Berwick; "it belongs to the old sea dog evidently. I suppose you want me to hold it, while you climb gracefully down."

"Hardly," mocked Jim. "I'd land so suddenly that it would drive my heels into my head. Here's a sliding window at the back here. Let's see how it looks below."

At the word, Jim pushed back the window and poking his head out took a good long look.

"Overhangs the water," exclaimed Jim as he pulled back.

"Let me have a peek," said the engineer, and looking down he saw the waves rushing in against the black rock of the cliff a hundred feet or more beneath. When the water withdrew there was a wet stretch of sandy cove, and then the waves came in with a foaming rush.

"It's pretty near high now," said Berwick, as he pulled his head in.

"I don't think it would be much of a trick to get around that projection of the cliff to the beach," remarked Jim.

"Maybe," replied Berwick noncommittally, with a slight shrug of his shoulders.

"You can swim like a fish," put in Jim who had noted the shrug of his comrade's shoulders.

"But I was thinking of you, my poor friend," replied the engineer. "What would become of you if the hungry ocean should seize upon you with its white and foaming teeth?"

"Oh, I'd wade out," remarked Jim nonchalantly.

"Humph," grunted Berwick; "by the way, Jim, I think I can find something of real interest here."

He got down on his knees and began very carefully to brush away with his hands the debris on the floor.

"You ain't lost that diamond ring I gave you?" questioned Jim in mock anxiety.

He, too, got down on the floor and began to dust for himself.

"I've found it," cried Berwick; "just get your hulk off this door."

Jim obeyed promptly, exclaiming, "Hully Gee, it's a trap!"

"What would you expect?" replied the engineer. "The captain could use this nicely in his line of trade I'm thinking."

"That is where that poor fellow would have been sent, whom we found in the gulch," exclaimed Jim.

"Certain thing," agreed his friend.

"I've got an idea," said Jim, lying flat on the floor. He stuck his head through the trap door while his friend held him solicitously by his legs so he could not do the sudden disappearance act.

"I can fix it," declared Jim as he pulled his head back; "just let me have the end of that rope."

The engineer did as requested, and Jim slipped the rope's end around one of the log joists and tied it securely.

"It will be a good thing to have this fastened here, in case we should have to come back," remarked Jim.

"Which I hope we won't until we get something to eat," said Berwick, who was not so young and enthusiastic as to find sufficient food in an adventure as Jim did.

"Might fish through here," remarked Jim.

"Yes, with a bent pin," replied the engineer caustically, "as far as getting anything to eat."

Jim laughed gleefully.

"Well, I'm off, or down rather," he said, his face growing sober. "You're next, Chief."

CHAPTER XXVIII

A SQUARE MEAL

However, before Jim began his descent, he cut off some of the rope.

"That might come in handy, you know," he said.

Then without any more adieu he let himself down, caught the edge of the trap, then dropped, seizing the rope and thus hand over hand until he was within a few feet of the water, then watching his chance as a wave receded, he dropped onto the sand and at top speed made around the projecting cliff. It extended, however, farther than he had thought, and the returning water caught him and it was only by his exerting himself to the utmost that he was able to grip a narrow outcrop of the rock from the face of the cliff. Instantly he thought of his comrade, who was much lighter than himself, and though he could swim it would not help him much against the fierce rush of the water. A little above him there was quite a wide ledge. This he gained as quickly as he could. Meanwhile John Berwick had let himself through the trap door, closing it down, and began his descent of the rope.

"Look out, John!" came Jim's voice from an unexpected quarter; "it's dangerous around that curve. I'll fling you a rope if you don't make it."

"Aye, aye, sir," cried the engineer; "here goes."

Then he dropped on the skirt of the retreating waves and dashed around the promontory, but the water coming back caught him. However, he got further than Jim because he was even quicker and more active. Nevertheless, the charging water clutched him all the more fiercely because of the nearness of his escape, and it took him up towards the beach side of the cliff.

"Catch it," yelled Jim, flinging him the rope.

But to his surprise and dismay, the engineer made no effort to seize the rope. Perhaps, thought Jim, he was already overcome, but this was not the case. Berwick, who was an excellent swimmer, had a plan of his own, for he was not bewildered or frightened and he had noted one or two things even as the wave caught him. He would not catch the rope flung to him because of the chance of dragging Jim off his perch in spite of the latter's great strength, and then, too, he was liable to be hurled against the cliff and be badly injured, so he let the wave carry him back, exerting himself so as to be brought nearer the beach on the return. Being a splendid swimmer, as has been said, he made it with a few yards to spare between the edge of the cliff and the sand. Jim drew a big sigh of relief when he saw his friend safe and prepared to get out of his own difficulty. He was able by careful climbing to edge and work his way down until at last he was within a twelve-foot leap of the beach. This he did with ease, lighting gently in the soft sand.

"Why, John, you look damp," he said as his friend joined him. "Been in swimming?"

"I always like to take a salt bath before eating," replied his friend; "gives you a relish for your dinner, you know."

"By Jove, if you are going to get any more relish for your meal, I will be hanged if I am going to pay for it," said Jim with a laugh.

"Come on," said Berwick, paying no attention to Jim's persiflage.

Away they trudged across the sandy beach towards the funny little restaurant of two cars where they had eaten the night before. Whatever surprise the stout German may have felt at seeing them altogether soaked and disguisedly dirty, and likewise alive, he showed none; he was strictly business.

"Vell, gentlemans, and vat vill you haf this time?" he inquired.

"Everything you've got," said Berwick shortly.

"A salad and after dinner coffee for my friend," put in Jim, "and I will take"—and here Jim enumerated a bill of fare that would have done credit to two men.

"The same for me," said the engineer, imperturbably, when James had finished his little spiel.

"I denk you gentlemens are hungry," said Herr Scheff, as he saw a chance to make a big profit.

"Mein Gottness!" it was the voice of Frau Scheff, "mein kindlins, you are drowned, poor tings, come, fix you fine and gute. You go ahead and cook dem blenty," she commanded her husband as she saw a frown on his forehead.

He knew that tone of voice and obeyed. The two comrades followed her into the cozy bedroom.

"I vill haf to give you mein Herr's clothes, it's all I haf," and she smiled broadly.

"Thank you, Frau Scheff," replied Jim; "while ours are getting dry it will give us more room to eat."

"Aye, dot is a true wort," and she laughed with a jolly, shaking heartiness.

It was comical beyond words when they made the change in clothing, while Frau Scheff had gone to the front to help her husband to prepare the meal for the two guests. The engineer, who was short, was almost lost in the voluminous trousers of mein host, and could have easily tied them around his neck, while another pair came to half mast on the long-legged Jim, and were much too large so that they flapped like a sail.

"Talk about dressing for dinner, John, you ought certainly to be pleased," said Jim with a grin.

"No time for humor," declared the engineer; "I am too weak to laugh."

At this saying, he tripped in his newly acquired garments and fell full length, and Jim over him. They were both so exhausted from laughing they could scarcely get up. Jim was the first to arise and he helped up the other "end man," for that was the character the two suggested to each other. When they got in the quaint restaurant car, the proprietor accepted their appearance with professional gravity, only growling under his breath, "It's a wonder Lena didn't let them have mein best suit."

What a repast the two comrades found on the little round table in the corner, covered with a snowy cloth! Two big thick tender steaks well garnished with potato salad, the handiwork of Frau Lena Scheff, creamed potatoes, huge cups of delicious coffee and a grand finale of broad, sugar-frosted, German pancakes.

By the time this feast was finished their own garments were thoroughly dry, and as lightning change artists they appeared in their own clothes, renewed in body as well as in appearance.

"We have fed and slept," said Berwick, "and ought to be ready for the next move."

"Herr Scheff," questioned Jim, "do you happen to know where we can get a good rowboat?"

This gave to his comrade some indication of what the next move would be.

"Yah! Yah! mein freund," replied the German, who felt as gracious as it was possible for him to feel. "You go down the beach haf a mile and you find a fisherman and him got two very nice boats."

Thanking their German acquaintance, they spoke a hearty good-by to Frau Scheff who bade them a cheerful and affectionate farewell, making them promise to come to the restaurant when they needed food, clothing or shelter. The two comrades started down the beach, continuing until they came to a sheltered cove where, in a small, ship-shape hut, they found a weazened old fisherman who regarded them with taciturn scrutiny when they told him what they wanted.

"For a couple of days you want my boat? All right, I charge

you five dollars."

Jim readily agreed to this.

"We haven't got much sense," exclaimed the engineer suddenly. "If we are going on a cruise we ought to have some provisions." Jim hit his skull a sound rap.

"Dunkerhead," he exclaimed. "I tell you, John, when we select the boat we will row up to Frau Scheff's and lay in a supply. That must have been my original plan, but I forgot it," concluded Jim brazenly.

Berwick threw back his head and laughed heartily.

"There is no getting away from it, Jim, you have a good opinion of yourself."

This gave Jim a certain shock as the expression of his face showed.

"I was only joshing," he said, and there was a slight sense of hurt in his tones that Berwick was quick to recognize.

"That's all right, old chap," he said, "your head is level."

This straightened out, they went and took a look at the old sailor's two boats in the cove. One was painted white with a red stripe, and the other was as black as a Venetian Gondola.

"That's a beauty," exclaimed Jim enthusiastically, looking at the lines of her, and he pointed to the black boat.

"She oughter be, I built her myself," said the old sailor, "and I know somethin' about boats, too."

"Got speed?" ejaculated Jim.

"Enough to burn a streak across this bay, boy."

Jim laughed good-naturedly, and the old sailor was evidently pleased with his appreciation.

CHAPTER XXIX

A REMINISCENCE

The bargain completed, the two comrades were about to board the craft when the old sailor of the cove interposed.

"I reckon you ain't in any sort of a hurry. If you start across the bay now before it gets plumb dark old Bill Broome is liable to ketch yer," and the aged fellow gave Jim a shrewd look from under his grizzled eyebrows.

"I guess that he wouldn't really do us any damage," replied Jim, with an assumed carelessness.

"I should think that you would have to look out for him, yourself," put in the engineer; "he's just as likely as not to drop in on you sometime, and take your two boats and such ballast as you have stowed away in your cabin, that he might take a fancy to."

"Him," said the old sailor with indescribable contempt; "why, old Bill wouldn't come within a mile of my cabin, unless he was drug here. I had quite a set-to with him a few years ago, and since thet time he don't even pass the time of day with me." He was quick to see that he had roused the deep interest of his two visitors. "Come in to my cabin, while

I smoke a pipe," he continued, "and I'll tell yer about that fracas between old Broome and myself."

"Certainly we will come in," said the engineer; "we are in no rush that I know of."

"Suits me," agreed Jim tersely.

They entered the cabin through a low doorway that caused Jim to stoop his proud crest as it were. The interior was snug and cozy with brown-hued walls and wooden beams that gave the room the appearance of a ship's cabin. A large lamp swung from the center of the ceiling gave a tempered light through a green shade.

There were several nautical prints upon the wall, and in front of a small stove, wherein glowed coals through its iron teeth, lay on a rug of woven rags a huge yellow cat stretched out at full and comfortable length. Everything was scrupulously neat about the place, and kept in ship-shape condition. The old man seated himself in a hacked wooden chair with semicircular arms and a green cushion. Jim took his place on a sea-chest, once green but now much faded, and with heavy rope handles, while the engineer occupied the other chair. After the sailor's wrinkled old wife had brought in some coffee for his two guests, and he had filled his short black pipe, he began his narrative of his once-time scrap with Captain William Broome, of unpious memory.

"That was one of the most unusual jobs I ever tackled when I took command of the *Storm King* for J. J. Singleton."

"That's the famous mining man, who used to live in San Francisco," remarked John Berwick.

"The same fellow," continued the old sailor, "and in spite of his money he had a lot of sensible ideas. You see, old 'J. J,' as he was known hereabouts, had three sons, the oldest seventeen, and their mother being dead for some years he brought 'em up according as he thought best. Had 'em work in one of his mines learning to run an engine and earning their own money. The youngest was on a big cattle ranch that the old man owned down in the southern part of the state.

"He told the boys that when they earned a certain amount they could put it into a steam yacht and what was lacking he would make up. Maybe those kids didn't work hard for some years until they had what was needed. I had been in command of one of Singleton's coasting ships and the old man picked me to take charge of the *Storm King*, which was the fool name of the yacht that they invested in, but there was nothing the matter with the boat herself.

"'Teach 'em navigating, Captain,' he says to me in his final instructions, 'and give 'em a taste of the rope's end if they ain't sharp to obey orders.'"

"But shucks, I had no trouble with them boys, they weren't like rich men's sons, but knew what hard work meant and could obey orders as well as give 'em. The oldest one's name was John—about your size," pointing to Jim, "but one of those sandy complected chaps, with white eyelashes and cool, gray eyes and no end of grit. The other two named Sam and Joe, were active, competent lads, and they had brought with them a friend off the cattle ranch, whom they called 'Comanche,' and I want you to know that boy was some shot with a revolver, rifle or cannon.

"Well, the second day out was where Captain Bill Broome put in an appearance. He was a smuggler and cutthroat in those days, and did a little kidnaping on the side."

"He hasn't reformed yet either," put in Jim.

"Not him," agreed the narrator; "he thought that he would make a rich haul on this occasion if he could get hold of the three Singleton boys and hold them for ransom. As soon as I saw the long, gray *Shark*, which I was quick to recognize, and noticed how she hung on our course, I knew what the game was and, as she had the speed on us, I saw that it was a case of fight or surrender. I can tell you it wasn't a pleasant situation for me. I felt my responsibility and I didn't want to face old Singleton if anything happened to those boys. I told 'em exactly what we was facing, and it would warm your heart to have seen the spirit they showed.

"The oldest one declared that their father would never give up one cent if they surrendered until their ship sank under 'em, and I guess the lad was right. Now we had three cannon aboard, a long, black, six pounder mounted aft, which the boys had named 'Black Tom,' and two smaller brass cannon forward on the bridge deck on either side. I had grinned at these guns when they were first taken aboard, considering that they were part of a kid game, and said to the old man that I wasn't qualified to command a man-of-war and that we might be able to trade the brass pieces for an island to some chief in the south seas, but now I saw that they might come in handy, and enable us to land a few kicks in old Bill's side even if he got us later, as was almost certain, for he was sure to have the range on us.

"I could see a long, wicked gun that the *Shark* carried forward, and there were three cannon on a side; these I could make out clearly through my glass. 'I'll navigate the ship,' I said to John Singleton, 'and you fight her.'"

"'Agreed to that, sir,' he answered, gripping my hand, and I was soon to learn that he was no kid at the fighting game either. It was now about eleven of a clear morning, with a smooth and slightly rolling sea; the *Shark* was drawing up slowly and steadily, and was about five miles astern.

"'I reckon it will be an hour and a half before she gets within range, Captain,' said John Singleton.

"'Just about that,' I replied, wondering how he had estimated it so closely, but he was one of the most practical chaps I ever saw.

"That will give us time for a good sound feed," remarked John. 'But I don't feel like eating, Jack,' protested his younger brother, Sam.

"'Sure you've got to eat, Sam,' replied John; 'this game isn't going to be anything like as fierce as what you and I have faced in the mining camp. Take my word for it, you won't be fit for anything unless you have a square meal.' I couldn't help but admire the way in which the lad put heart into his brothers, and I felt confident that he would more than hold his end up when it came to the fighting. However, it seemed to me, the contest could end only one way and as a forlorn hope, I steered southwest on the chance of cutting across the course of one of the Pacific steamers, but all I succeeded in raising was the sail of a Borkentine low down to the south and a few points west.

"About half past two that afternoon the trouble began. The *Shark* was nearing the half-mile limit; a long, gray boat of iron, built for speed and stripped of all superfluous tackle.

"'They are getting ready to show their teeth,' remarked John, pointing to a group of three men in the bow.

"Besides the men in the bow of the *Shark*, there were several in the waist leaning over the rail and sizing up the *Storm King* with cold and calculating eyes.

"'Let's give 'em a shot, John,' I heard Joe urge.

"'No hurry,' replied his brother; 'don't let them worry you into wasting any ammunition.'"

"In a few minutes John Singleton turned to me, 'could you turn her course a few points to the north, Captain?' he asked.

"'Certainly,' I replied.

"'Thank you,' responded the lad, 'I've a plan and it won't take over five minutes.'"

"Then he and his friend, Comanche, lowered one of the ship's boats on the starboard side, where it was sheltered from the sight of the enemy by the deck cabins just abaft the midships. In this boat were two rifles, heavily loaded and ready for action. What the boy's scheme was I did not foresee but it was to develop a short time later.

"Upon the quarter deck of the *Shark* paced the figure of Captain Broome, with his long, swinging gorilla-like arms. Suddenly he stopped, put his hand to his mouth and shouted an order to the men in the bow of the ship. Then came the quick move of one of the men. A flash leaped from the mouth of the forward gun, a dull detonation, and a white cloud of smoke curled back over the bow of the *Shark*, while the shell plunged into the water directly in front of our prow.

"'That's for us to heave to,' cried John; 'give him our answer, Comanche, and give it to him hard!'

"Comanche obeyed with belligerent willingness, and with an

accuracy of aim that was utterly surprising to old Bill Broome, for the round shot struck his boat amidship, and it fell back into the water. The distance was too great to do execution, but a yell of triumph went up from the boys on the deck of the *Storm King*.

"'Just a little higher next time,' cried Jack Singleton; 'sweep the rascal's decks for him.'"

"It was good advice and now the fight was on, and it was like a real naval engagement, with the constant bark of the guns, the heavy clouds of white sulphurous smoke rolling over the quiet sea between the combatants, and the thrusting flames from the mouths of the guns flashing into the smoke. But the fire of the enemy was becoming more accurate and deadly, and it was a question of only a few minutes before a well-directed shot would completely disable us.

"'Pull down our flag, Captain,' yelled John Singleton; 'let him come alongside.'"

"It seemed to me the only thing to do, and in a couple of minutes the long gray *Shark* had slipped through the smoke on our portside. Old Bill could not resist the temptation to make some remarks before he boarded us.

"'I'd like to know, Cap'n, what you, and your parcel of kids mean by attacking me on the high seas, me going along peaceable, just enjoying a fishin' cruise for my health. I'll take it out of yer blasted hide for making me this trouble, and I'll baste them pretty boys of your'n to a finish, or my name ain't Bill Broome!'

"'Which it ain't,' I says, and I proceeded to hand him out a line of talk that kept him eager to say something else about my character.

"You see I noticed that John and Comanche had disappeared just as the *Shark* hove alongside, and I intended to give them all the time I could, and I could of yelled when I see'd John creeping up behind the Cap'n; and the next second he had felled him with the butt of his rifle, and Comanche had done the same for two of the men who were standing in the waist of the ship, joining in our previous conversation.

"Well, it wasn't ten seconds before I was aboard with four of my crew and it was no time before we had possession of that ship. Now you see the purpose of John Singleton in lowering the boat when he did. He had used it to slip around the stern of the *Shark* and to slip up on Bill Broome and his crew."

"Great work," cried Jim, in admiration, "but what did you do with 'em when you had them caught?"

"That didn't bother us long," said the old fellow; "we didn't want their company, and we had to fix it so they wouldn't bother us, so we put their engines out of commission, so they had to use their small sails; broke their cannons, and threw all their ammunition into the sea, and left them, to their own devices."

"Where is the *Storm King* and her crew now, Captain?" asked the engineer with evident interest.

"Cruising down in the South Seas, I reckon."

"Some time we may run across them, eh, Chief?" questioned Jim.

"Stranger things have happened," replied Berwick with a knowing grin.

"Well, I don't intend to let John Singleton beat me at the

game with our mutual friend, Captain Broome," remarked Jim, as he rose to his feet.

"The old chap was right enough," remarked Jim, as the two of them sent the beautiful boat over the slightly rolling waters of the gray, sodden-hued bay towards Frau Scheff's. "If money can buy her, I am going to own this boat. There is no telling when we might find use for her, if we ever go down into the South Seas."

"You want something bigger than this low, black, rakish craft if you are going to be a pirate in the South Seas," remarked Berwick caustically.

"Indeed, yes!" agreed Jim. "I'm sure going to have the *Sea Eagle* over yonder," and he nodded his head in the direction of the open bay.

"When Captain Broome gets done with her?" questioned Berwick slyly.

"Perhaps sooner; I dunno," said Jim gloomily.

They beached their long, low, black craft on the sands below the restaurant of Herr and Frau Scheff, and from that base of supplies laid in a liberal stock of provisions, enough to last for a day at least. There was some ham, a loaf of bread, butter and an apple pie. Sauerkraut they had to politely refuse, for, as Jim said in an aside to his friend, "There was no disguising their trail from the enemy if they carried that." But they had plenty of other necessities, including tea and coffee. They were also loaned a few necessary cooking utensils, and thus equipped, they launched out in their skiff once more.

CHAPTER XXX

JIM BOARDS THE PIRATE

"Whither away, Brother?" questioned John Berwick, as they bent gently and rhythmically to the oars.

"I thought we might lay alongside the *Sea Eagle*, and invite Brother Broome to surrender," suggested Jim.

"All right, I'm with you, as I can't walk ashore," replied John Berwick.

However, instead of rowing straight in the direction of the *Sea Eagle*, Jim bent a circuitous course around her. It was now growing towards evening and a heavy fog was rolling in even then over the sea towards the Golden Gate. The two comrades in a short time reached the western shore of the bay near which the *Sea Eagle* lay anchored.

Here they rowed slowly along, looking for some place to camp. At first the shore was high and rocky, but after rowing for nearly a mile they came to a small inlet where a tiny stream trickled down from a hidden spring above in the woods. There were pines and sycamore trees both, and altogether it was a delightful place for a camp. Jim's trained eye took it all in at a glance.

"Here's where we haul in, John," he said.

"It looks good to me," agreed Berwick.

Indeed, it was an excellent place, well sheltered, and with good water. The rest they had with them.

"What time are you going to make your attack, Jim, my boy?" asked Berwick.

"I fancy any time between eleven and one would do," said Jim. "That will give us time to get in a couple of hours' sleep at least. It's just as well to store up a little rest. There is no telling what will happen; when we once get started it may be a week before we get another chance."

"Correct," said Berwick; "which watch shall I take, Captain?"

"The first," said Jim, "if you don't mind."

"But I do mind," said Berwick quickly, "when I'm told."

While Jim sat watching some hours later, with everything quiet except the gentle lapping of the water along the rocky shore, his mind reverted to the incidents of the past few hours, but quickly changed to the distant scene of his home.

"I wish I had Jo and Tom with me, and Juarez, too; it looks to me as though there was going to be a change of scene soon, and then we will need 'em by way of reenforcements." He brooded thus to himself over his home folks and the chances of the future until it was time for them to reconnoiter the enemy if nothing else was done. "I have given John three-quarters of an hour longer than he expected," he said as he looked at his watch. "It is now a quarter of twelve."

Berwick responded promptly to the call of time.

"Jove!" he said, "I don't see how you can pick up the *Sea Eagle* or anything else in such thick weather."

"It would not be easy if we struck out direct from this inlet," replied Jim, "but I'm going to keep along the shore to a point that I made a note of coming in, and then row direct out; we can't lose her."

They did accordingly, but they had to row very slowly, so that Jim could be able to make out his landmark.

"There it is," he said. "See, here is a point of rock that juts out; there is no mistaking it."

"What is your plan?" asked the engineer.

"There is only one thing to do," replied Jim; "we are not taking this exercise for our health. We will drop along the *Sea Eagle*, board her, find where the senorita is, and row her ashore."

"Are you sure she is on the yacht?" queried Berwick.

"Nowhere else," replied Jim stoutly. "You don't suppose that old Broome would leave her in the castle after the alarm we raised. The reason he didn't search for us around the premises was because he had gone off to hide on the *Sea Eagle*."

Nothing more was said, and they rowed slowly from the point of departure until they saw the faint loom of the *Sea Eagle* through the night and fog. There was a light astern and two forward, one on the starboard and the other on the port, while a fourth shed a dim light from the masthead.

There was no sound, whatever, and no figure in sight, which was not remarkable, considering you could see no distance whatever on account of the thick fog, but Jim was seaman enough to know that there was sure to be someone on the bridge, and a watch forward. Berwick brought the boat gently along the side near the stern rail and Jim was aboard in a jiffy. Then the engineer pushed off for a few feet where he and the black boat could not be seen, and waited in ambush for what might happen. He believed that Jim stood a good chance to rescue the senorita, a much better chance, in fact, than when she was held captive in the castle. Once get her into the boat and they, too, would make sure of her safety.

Jim felt a thrill as he once more set foot on the well-known deck. He felt strong enough to take her back single-handed, and what would he not have given to be on the bridge again, with Jo and the rest of the old crew on deck, and the *Sea Eagle* pushing her nose out through the Golden Gate, heading for the enchanted regions of the tropic seas.

But Jim took only a moment for such romancing. There was grim and hard work ahead before he could ever be master of his own boat again. He knew the ship as a hand does a glove, and in this there was a great advantage. He cautiously tried the doors of the staterooms on the upper deck. In one he made out the lean figure of the second mate in his bunk, sound asleep. At that moment he saw the door of the captain's cabin open. Jim glided aft and crouched low near the capstan, where he was hard to be distinguished from a coil of rope.

He saw the squat figure of Captain Broome with the long, swinging, gorilla-like arms revealed in the light which shone from the interior of the cabin, and then he slammed the door and strolled forward towards the bridge. Jim held his breath, hoping he would not come his way.

When the old pirate had disappeared, Jim completed his search of the deck staterooms, but the senorita was in none of them. The only thing that remained for Jim was to search the rooms leading from the main saloon below. He rather mistrusted going down there, and he had most sincerely hoped that the girl would be in one of the deck rooms, then his task would have been comparatively easy, but it seemed as if luck was breaking against him.

He went cautiously but quickly along the deck until he reached the stairway leading down into the cabin. There was the large lamp lit in the saloon, but turned very low. As he cautiously descended into the saloon his heart went into his throat at the sight of the gaunt woman with the red hair who had been the senorita's jailer in the castle. She was apparently asleep on one of the divans, but Jim would have much rather seen anyone else on guard than this redoubtable woman whose vigilance had been his undoing before. It might have been possible to have outwitted or defeated a man, but he really was in some awe of this Amazon.

The first thing for Jim to do was to determine which of the four cabins opening off the saloon was the prison of the senorita. He could not go from one to the other opening the doors, for the woman on guard would be sure to hear, nor could he say after the manner of children, "My mother told me to take this one."

It was like the suitor of Portia in the "Merchant of Venice," who was forced to choose his fate from one of three chests with misleading mottoes on them. But there was no time to lose. Should he take a chance? There seemed no other way. However, Jim was an experienced scout, as the reader well knows, and his skill could be put to use inside of walls as well as out on the desert or in the pathless mountains, where he might be searching for some obscure trail.

He crawled over the heavily carpeted floor on his hands and knees to the first door, but he found no trace to guide him. The second seemed to reward his scrutiny, for the nap of the rug showed the imprint of feet and the brass knob of the door was somewhat tarnished.

At that moment he heard the sound of heavy feet upon the stairway. He knew that tread; he had heard it before. There was no hiding-place except under the hanging of the heavy tablecloth, and with a quiet celerity, Jim slid under its protection just as the woman stirred from the divan, and then the captain's heavy, growling voice made itself heard as he came down into the saloon.

"I'm going to pull anchor out of here to-morrow, Ann," said the skipper; "it's jest about time."

"What hour, Brother?" asked the woman.

This startled Jim, who had not guessed that this woman was any relation of the redoubtable Bill Broome, and that so human a word as "Brother" could be applied to the old pirate had never entered his head. This rawboned woman was quite the equal of her brother, and her life had brought out that hardness and cruelty that is latent only too often in the New England character.

To her question the captain replied, "Not later than four if we are to get clear. I'm going into Frisco on a little business first."

"Do we take the gal?" questioned the woman, following his thought in some obscure way.

"Then she is here," mused Jim.

"Part way, anyhow," he rumbled in his harsh voice. "Every day of bother getting rid of her brings up her price."

Jim felt the hot blood of rage warm the roots of his hair. The cold-blooded cruelty and calculation of it made him long to get hold of the old codger. Perhaps he would in a moment.

"Git me something to eat, Ann, old gal," he said. "I'd better begin to lay in ballast for to-morrow."

The captain took his seat at the table, and put his feet squarely on the unsuspected Jim. Then came the explosion.

"By tarnation thunder, there's somebody under thar," he exclaimed, rising to his feet.

Jim crawled from under as quick as he could, and with a sense of sullen fury he saw the game was up for a second time. If he had cared to escape without striking a blow he did not have a chance. As he emerged the captain was on his back with all the ferocity of a hyena.

"It's that blasted young beggar again," he yelled. "We'll do him good this time."

Wyn Roosevelt

CHAPTER XXXI

THE END, A NEW START

Jim, well fed and rested, was up to his full strength, and to this was added his fierce anger against the captain. Not on his own personal account, but because of his heartless cruelty towards the captive girl whom he had in his power and was holding for ransom. With a twist Jim got hold of the back of Captain Bill Broome's neck, and by means of a mighty wrench he got the old wretch around in front of him, breaking free from his hold. Jim sent him staggering back.

As the captain, regaining his footing, rushed forward like an enraged bull, Jim Darlington measured him with a crashing blow on the jaw that sent him dazed against a sharp edge of woodwork that cut his scalp and laid him out for the moment. Drawn by the racket, the first and second mate came tumbling down, and joined in the attack, but Jim knew a trick or two about boxing and surprised them with lightning blows that they did not know how to block. He was hampered, however, by a lack of space. Nevertheless, as they came to close quarters, jarred and bleeding, Jim was able to fling them off, the sinews of his powerful frame working in perfect unison.

Just at the moment he was free, he stumbled over the

prostrate body of the captain, who thus accomplished more by his prone position than when he was on his feet and in the midst of the fray. At this juncture, the Amazon sister jumped into the fight. She had run up on deck for a purpose, when the fight started, and returned with a marlin spike. Jim was so involved with the two mates for a few brief seconds that he did not see her, and would not have paid much attention if he had, he was so full of the struggle in hand.

As Jim stumbled, before he could regain his feet, the woman brought down the marlin spike with a glancing blow on the side of his head. The boy dropped as though dead. There was no doubt of the strength of the captain's sister. She was evidently more than a match for any man aboard, and it was little wonder that the youth lay like a log, the blood streaming from a cut on the side of his head. He had not heard the shriek of the senorita as she threw open the door of her cabin prison and saw Jim lying almost at her feet.

As she stooped to his help (she was no hysterical girl to faint at the sight of blood), she was thrust violently back, after a short struggle, by the captain's sister, and locked in the cabin. However, she did not weep or wring her hands, but she became suddenly, even ominously quiet, her eyes shining in the pallor of her face with a luminous light. Meanwhile, there was a council of war outside in the cabin as to the disposal of their prostrate enemy.

Old Captain Broome had recovered enough to enable him to stand up, holding on to the table, but he was still swaying somewhat, and was an ugly looking customer with his cut face.

"Better put him in the hold until we get out to sea," said the Amazon sister.

"I reckon he's done for this time," said the captain; "he oughter be if you gave him one of your love taps, Anne," he concluded, with a ghastly grin.

The woman bent down and coolly felt the boy's pulse, and pushed back the lids of his eyes, with no more show of feeling than if he had not been a human being.

"He ain't quite done for," she said, getting to her feet.

"Then he will be, durn soon," declared the old captain venomously. "Here, Bill, you and Gus take him up on deck and throw him over. That sure will finish him. One of you take his feet and t'other his head, and Ann will give you a hist up the stairs. I'm too joggled to help any, but I will give him my blessing as he goes over, that is, if you don't feel too squeamish to do it."

The two mates laughed at this with great heartiness.

"I will say this for that young feller, he was some fighter," remarked Bill. "I have handled some hard specimens in my time, but he was the toughest yet. He handed me and Gus a couple of cuffs that made our jaws wobble."

They got the limp figure up the stairs with the Amazon's help, but she did not follow, but went below to get her brother something to eat as his strenuous day had begun, and he stood in need of immediate ballast. The scene just enacted might have been a daily occurrence from her perfect indifference, as indeed scenes of violence no doubt were, but none of the men could equal her in *sangfroid*.

Now they were on deck. Which way would they turn, to the right or left rail. They did not know it, but it would make all the difference in the world which side they would choose.

"I tell you, boys, you can throw him overboard in front of my cabin; that would just suit me to the ground," said the captain.

"Aye, aye, sir," replied the amiable pair of mates.

It was accomplished in short order. There was a heave of the shoulders, and then a heavy splash into the dark waters beneath. No one heard or heeded a low wailing cry from the prisoner in the cabin. She knew what had happened. She flung the small port hole open as Jim fell and the water from the impact splashed into her face. Then to her unspeakable relief she saw a black boat glide to where the figure came up, and she saw that he was in safe hands.

With a quick motion she knotted her daintily-scented handkerchief and tossed it into the boat as it swept by. It had her monogram on it, and the engineer was quick to seize the handkerchief as well as the import of it.

"I will give it to him, Senorita," he said in a low voice. Then the boat was one with the darkness, and was gone from her sight, but she was happy knowing that Jim was safe. She was not thinking of herself and her own danger at the time, as is the way of some women.

John Berwick, the engineer, had had an anxious time while Jim had been conducting his seance on board the ship, and it was his prompt action that had saved his friend. It was some luck, too, that the three rascals aboard had not sighted the slender dark boat, but they were dazed somewhat, due to the effect of Jim's fierce attack upon them, and likewise the two comrades deserved a little luck considering how fortunate their enemies had been of late.

Berwick lost no time in pulling for the shore, and had no

difficulty in finding the outjutting rock which was the point of departure.

* * * * *

It was a full two hours before Berwick could bring Jim fully around, and then the latter sat by a bright camp fire in the cove, pale and drawn, with a handkerchief tied around his injured head. He was drinking some coffee, but as yet he could not eat anything.

"Who was the guy, John, who first called women the weaker sex?" inquired Jim, in a faint and injured tone.

"Some chump who probably died a sadder and a wiser man," replied his friend.

"I only wish the gentle Annie back there had given him a tap with the shillalah," remarked Jim.

Finally, by the time the fog thickened, Jim was himself once more and the two comrades had determined upon their course. They had this advantage in that they knew, from what Jim had overheard, something of the immediate plans of Captain Bill Broome and his evil crew, and what actually occurred will be fully and graphically told in the "Frontier Boys in the South Seas." Furthermore, at this particular time, the captain believed his enemy drowned beyond all possibility of a doubt; therefore, he would not be on his guard against him in the future, and would know of no need to hurry his departure.

"All aboard now, John," said Jim. He rose stiffly to his feet. "We will row across the bay to the city and charter a fast craft to follow these beggars. I guess there will be a surprise in store for those blooming pirates in a few days."

"We are short of cash, Captain," remarked John; "I don't see how we are going to get a boat."

"Trust to luck," said Jim; "it is coming our way I tell you. That was the break when I wasn't drowned this morning."

It came out, the luck part, as Jim said, and yet it was nothing so remarkable, for as they had rowed some distance on their way and were between the shore and the *Sea Eagle*, John Berwick suddenly stopped at a gesture from Jim.

"Hold on," he whispered, "there is a boat coming our way."

Sure enough, in half a minute a rapidly propelled boat shot into their circle of the fog. It was pulled by two powerful Hawaiians and heading for the *Sea Eagle*. In the stern sat the humped and well-known and sinister figure of the Mexican dwarf.

"Halt, there," cried Jim. The two Hawaiians obeyed with indifferent good nature.

"None of that, Manuel," yelled Jim, as the Mexican started to draw, and himself leveling a revolver which they had captured in the castle. It is true it had but one cartridge in it, but that was enough with Jim at the directing end of it.

The Mexican wilted as he saw the game was up, and his transfer was quickly made. Then Jim after a hasty and vigorous search, with a yell of triumph, unbuckled his treasure belt which the Mexican had stolen from, him on the train.

"What did I tell you about our luck, John, old boy?" cried Jim. "You boys come along with us," he continued, speaking to the Hawaiians; "we give you good pay and treat you right."

"Yes, yes," they agreed smilingly, adding, "Wele ke hau." This was their native phrase of enthusiasm; in other words, their college yell.

So they took the place of the oarsmen in the black boat, and trailed the other behind. They rowed with splendid speed and precision towards the city. The Mexican laid in the bottom of the boat at Jim's feet, securely tied. The tables were turned, indeed.

I need not weary you with the business details by which Jim Darlington and the engineer got the boat they wanted, nor how they were joined by Tom, Jo and Juarez, but at three o'clock one fair day the *Sea Eagle* glided gracefully through the Golden Gate and turned her prow to the southwest, and in due time thereafter a slender but powerfully engined black boat slipped through to the open sea and on the trail.

And now, Jim Darlington, and your crew, the best of good luck go with you, for we know you all of old, and we like you. Vale.

Choose from Thousands of 1stWorldLibrary Classics By

A. M. Barnard
Ada Leverson
Adolphus William Ward
Aesop
Agatha Christie
Alexander Aaronsohn
Alexander Kielland
Alexandre Dumas
Alfred Gatty
Alfred Ollivant
Alice Duer Miller
Alice Turner Curtis
Alice Dunbar
Allen Chapman
Alleyne Ireland
Ambrose Bierce
Amelia E. Barr
Amory H. Bradford
Andrew Lang
Andrew McFarland Davis
Andy Adams
Angela Brazil
Anna Alice Chapin
Anna Sewell
Annie Besant
Annie Hamilton Donnell
Annie Payson Call
Annie Roe Carr
Annonaymous
Anton Chekhov
Archibald Lee Fletcher
Arnold Bennett
Arthur C. Benson
Arthur Conan Doyle
Arthur M. Winfield
Arthur Ransome
Arthur Schnitzler
Arthur Train
Atticus
B.H. Baden-Powell
B. M. Bower
B. C. Chatterjee
Baroness Emmuska Orczy
Baroness Orczy
Basil King
Bayard Taylor
Ben Macomber
Bertha Muzzy Bower
Bjornstjerne Bjornson

Booth Tarkington
Boyd Cable
Bram Stoker
C. Collodi
C. E. Orr
C. M. Ingleby
Carolyn Wells
Catherine Parr Traill
Charles A. Eastman
Charles Amory Beach
Charles Dickens
Charles Dudley Warner
Charles Farrar Browne
Charles Ives
Charles Kingsley
Charles Klein
Charles Hanson Towne
Charles Lathrop Pack
Charles Romyn Dake
Charles Whibley
Charles Willing Beale
Charlotte M. Braeme
Charlotte M. Yonge
Charlotte Perkins Stetson
Clair W. Hayes
Clarence Day Jr.
Clarence E. Mulford
Clemence Housman
Confucius
Coningsby Dawson
Cornelis DeWitt Wilcox
Cyril Burleigh
D. H. Lawrence
Daniel Defoe
David Garnett
Dinah Craik
Don Carlos Janes
Donald Keyhoe
Dorothy Kilner
Dougan Clark
Douglas Fairbanks
E. Nesbit
E. P. Roe
E. Phillips Oppenheim
E. S. Brooks
Earl Barnes
Edgar Rice Burroughs
Edith Van Dyne
Edith Wharton

Edward Everett Hale
Edward J. O'Biren
Edward S. Ellis
Edwin L. Arnold
Eleanor Atkins
Eleanor Hallowell Abbott
Eliot Gregory
Elizabeth Gaskell
Elizabeth McCracken
Elizabeth Von Arnim
Ellem Key
Emerson Hough
Emilie F. Carlen
Emily Bronte
Emily Dickinson
Enid Bagnold
Enilor Macartney Lane
Erasmus W. Jones
Ernie Howard Pie
Ethel May Dell
Ethel Turner
Ethel Watts Mumford
Eugene Sue
Eugenie Foa
Eugene Wood
Eustace Hale Ball
Evelyn Everett-green
Everard Cotes
F. H. Cheley
F. J. Cross
F. Marion Crawford
Fannie E. Newberry
Federick Austin Ogg
Ferdinand Ossendowski
Fergus Hume
Florence A. Kilpatrick
Fremont B. Deering
Francis Bacon
Francis Darwin
Frances Hodgson Burnett
Frances Parkinson Keyes
Frank Gee Patchin
Frank Harris
Frank Jewett Mather
Frank L. Packard
Frank V. Webster
Frederic Stewart Isham
Frederick Trevor Hill
Frederick Winslow Taylor

Friedrich Kerst
Friedrich Nietzsche
Fyodor Dostoyevsky
G.A. Henty
G.K. Chesterton
Gabrielle E. Jackson
Garrett P. Serviss
Gaston Leroux
George A. Warren
George Ade
Geroge Bernard Shaw
George Cary Eggleston
George Durston
George Ebers
George Eliot
George Gissing
George MacDonald
George Meredith
George Orwell
George Sylvester Viereck
George Tucker
George W. Cable
George Wharton James
Gertrude Atherton
Gordon Casserly
Grace E. King
Grace Gallatin
Grace Greenwood
Grant Allen
Guillermo A. Sherwell
Gulielma Zollinger
Gustav Flaubert
H. A. Cody
H. B. Irving
H. C. Bailey
H. G. Wells
H. H. Munro
H. Irving Hancock
H. R. Naylor
H. Rider Haggard
H. W. C. Davis
Haldeman Julius
Hall Caine
Hamilton Wright Mabie
Hans Christian Andersen
Harold Avery
Harold McGrath
Harriet Beecher Stowe
Harry Castlemon
Harry Coghill
Harry Houidini

Hayden Carruth
Helent Hunt Jackson
Helen Nicolay
Hendrik Conscience
Hendy David Thoreau
Henri Barbusse
Henrik Ibsen
Henry Adams
Henry Ford
Henry Frost
Henry James
Henry Jones Ford
Henry Seton Merriman
Henry W Longfellow
Herbert A. Giles
Herbert Carter
Herbert N. Casson
Herman Hesse
Hildegard G. Frey
Homer
Honore De Balzac
Horace B. Day
Horace Walpole
Horatio Alger Jr.
Howard Pyle
Howard R. Garis
Hugh Lofting
Hugh Walpole
Humphry Ward
Ian Maclaren
Inez Haynes Gillmore
Irving Bacheller
Isabel Cecilia Williams
Isabel Hornibrook
Israel Abrahams
Ivan Turgenev
J. G.Austin
J. Henri Fabre
J. M. Barrie
J. M. Walsh
J. Macdonald Oxley
J. R. Miller
J. S. Fletcher
J. S. Knowles
J. Storer Clouston
J. W. Duffield
Jack London
Jacob Abbott
James Allen
James Andrews
James Baldwin

James Branch Cabell
James DeMille
James Joyce
James Lane Allen
James Lane Allen
James Oliver Curwood
James Oppenheim
James Otis
James R. Driscoll
Jane Abbott
Jane Austen
Jane L. Stewart
Janet Aldridge
Jens Peter Jacobsen
Jerome K. Jerome
Jessie Graham Flower
John Buchan
John Burroughs
John Cournos
John F. Kennedy
John Gay
John Glasworthy
John Habberton
John Joy Bell
John Kendrick Bangs
John Milton
John Philip Sousa
John Taintor Foote
Jonas Lauritz Idemil Lie
Jonathan Swift
Joseph A. Altsheler
Joseph Carey
Joseph Conrad
Joseph E. Badger Jr
Joseph Hergesheimer
Joseph Jacobs
Jules Vernes
Julian Hawthrone
Julie A Lippmann
Justin Huntly McCarthy
Kakuzo Okakura
Karle Wilson Baker
Kate Chopin
Kenneth Grahame
Kenneth McGaffey
Kate Langley Bosher
Kate Langley Bosher
Katherine Cecil Thurston
Katherine Stokes
L. A. Abbot
L. T. Meade

L. Frank Baum	Paul G. Tomlinson	T. S. Arthur
Latta Griswold	Paul Severing	The Princess Der Ling
Laura Dent Crane	Percy Brebner	Thomas A. Janvier
Laura Lee Hope	Percy Keese Fitzhugh	Thomas A Kempis
Laurence Housman	Peter B. Kyne	Thomas Anderton
Lawrence Beasley	Plato	Thomas Bailey Aldrich
Leo Tolstoy	Quincy Allen	Thomas Bulfinch
Leonid Andreyev	R. Derby Holmes	Thomas De Quincey
Lewis Carroll	R. L. Stevenson	Thomas Dixon
Lewis Sperry Chafer	R. S. Ball	Thomas H. Huxley
Lilian Bell	Rabindranath Tagore	Thomas Hardy
Lloyd Osbourne	Rahul Alvares	Thomas More
Louis Hughes	Ralph Bonehill	Thornton W. Burgess
Louis Joseph Vance	Ralph Henry Barbour	U. S. Grant
Louis Tracy	Ralph Victor	Upton Sinclair
Louisa May Alcott	Ralph Waldo Emmerson	Valentine Williams
Lucy Fitch Perkins	Rene Descartes	Various Authors
Lucy Maud Montgomery	Ray Cummings	Vaughan Kester
Luther Benson	Rex Beach	Victor Appleton
Lydia Miller Middleton	Rex E. Beach	Victor G. Durham
Lyndon Orr	Richard Harding Davis	Victoria Cross
M. Corvus	Richard Jefferies	Virginia Woolf
M. H. Adams	Richard Le Gallienne	Wadsworth Camp
Margaret E. Sangster	Robert Barr	Walter Camp
Margret Howth	Robert Frost	Walter Scott
Margaret Vandercook	Robert Gordon Anderson	Washington Irving
Margaret W. Hungerford	Robert L. Drake	Wilbur Lawton
Margret Penrose	Robert Lansing	Wilkie Collins
Maria Edgeworth	Robert Lynd	Willa Cather
Maria Thompson Daviess	Robert Michael Ballantyne	Willard F. Baker
Mariano Azuela	Robert W. Chambers	William Dean Howells
Marion Polk Angellotti	Rosa Nouchette Carey	William le Queux
Mark Overton	Rudyard Kipling	W. Makepeace Thackeray
Mark Twain	Saint Augustine	William W. Walter
Mary Austin	Samuel B. Allison	William Shakespeare
Mary Catherine Crowley	Samuel Hopkins Adams	Winston Churchill
Mary Cole	Sarah Bernhardt	Yei Theodora Ozaki
Mary Hastings Bradley	Sarah C. Hallowell	Yogi Ramacharaka
Mary Roberts Rinehart	Selma Lagerlof	Young E. Allison
Mary Rowlandson	Sherwood Anderson	Zane Grey
M. Wollstonecraft Shelley	Sigmund Freud	
Maud Lindsay	Standish O'Grady	
Max Beerbohm	Stanley Weyman	
Myra Kelly	Stella Benson	
Nathaniel Hawthrone	Stella M. Francis	
Nicolo Machiavelli	Stephen Crane	
O. F. Walton	Stewart Edward White	
Oscar Wilde	Stijn Streuvels	
Owen Johnson	Swami Abhedananda	
P.G. Wodehouse	Swami Parmananda	
Paul and Mabel Thorne	T. S. Ackland	

www.ingramcontent.com/pod-product-compliance
Lightning Source LLC
Chambersburg PA
CBHW030313180626
46810CB00003B/1061